The Bonny Dawn

OTHER BOOKS BY
CATHERINE COOKSON

NOVELS

Kate Hannigan
The Fifteen Streets
Colour Blind
Maggie Rowan
Rooney
The Menagerie
Slinky Jane
Fanny McBride
Fenwick Houses
Heritage of Folly
The Garment
The Fen Tiger
The Blind Miller
House of Men
Hannah Massey
The Long Corridor
The Unbaited Trap
Katie Mulholland
The Round Tower
The Nice Bloke
The Glass Virgin
The Invitation
The Dwelling Place
Feathers in the Fire
Pure as the Lily
The Mallen Streak
The Mallen Girl
The Mallen Litter
The Invisible Cord
The Gambling Man
The Tide of Life
The Slow Awakening
The Iron Façade
The Girl

The Cinder Path
Miss Martha Mary Crawford
The Man Who Cried
Tilly Trotter
Tilly Trotter Wed
Tilly Trotter Widowed
The Whip
Hamilton
The Black Velvet Gown
Goodbye Hamilton
A Dinner of Herbs
Harold
The Moth
Bill Bailey
The Parson's Daughter
Bill Bailey's Lot
The Cultured Handmaiden
Bill Bailey's Daughter
The Harrogate Secret
The Black Candle
The Wingless Bird
The Gillyvors
My Beloved Son
The Rag Nymph
The House of Women
The Maltese Angel
The Year of the Virgins
The Golden Straw
Justice is a Woman
The Tinker's Girl
A Ruthless Need
The Obsession
The Upstart
The Branded Man

THE MARY ANN STORIES

A Grand Man
The Lord and Mary Ann
The Devil and Mary Ann
Love and Mary Ann

Life and Mary Ann
Marriage and Mary Ann
Mary Ann's Angels
Mary Ann and Bill

FOR CHILDREN

Matty Doolin
Joe and the Gladiator
The Nipper
Rory's Fortune
Our John Willie

Mrs Flannagan's Trumpet
Go Tell It To Mrs Golightly
Lanky Jones
Nancy Nutall and the Mongrel
Bill and the Mary Ann Shaughnessy

AUTOBIOGRAPHY

Our Kate
Catherine Cookson Country

Let Me Make Myself Plain
Plainer Still

CATHERINE COOKSON

The Bonny Dawn

BANTAM PRESS

LONDON · NEW YORK · TORONTO · SYDNEY · AUCKLAND

TRANSWORLD PUBLISHERS LTD
61–63 Uxbridge Road, London W5 5SA

TRANSWORLD PUBLISHERS (AUSTRALIA) PTY LTD
15–25 Helles Avenue, Moorebank, NSW 2170

TRANSWORLD PUBLISHERS (NZ) LTD
3 William Pickering Drive, Albany, Auckland

Published 1996 by Bantam Press
a division of Transworld Publishers Ltd
Copyright © Catherine Cookson 1996

A catalogue record for this book
is available from the British Library.

ISBN 0593 040929

Typeset in 11/14pt Sabon by
Hewer Text Composition Services, Edinburgh.
Printed in Great Britain by
Mackays of Chatham plc, Chatham, Kent.

One

THE ALARM WENT OFF IN THE MIDDLE OF HER dream. She was dreaming she was dancing, not the twist or jiving – these were beginning to be considered old-fashioned at the club – but something more old-fashioned still: she was gliding to music that seemed to come out of the clouds, for there was no orchestra that she could see and no roof to the ballroom. She knew there was a clear glass floor and she could see her legs reflected in it, but not those of her partner. She knew she was dancing with a man and that she liked him, but when she looked at the floor she could see no partner. It was as a feeling of keen disappointment was penetrating her dream that the alarm went off. It brought her spiralling up from the glass floor, through the roofless room and on to the bed, where she clutched wildly at the pillow. Pushing her hands underneath it, she swiftly switched off the muffled tinkling, then turned on her back and lay gasping, her eyes wide, staring upwards into the darkness while her ears strained towards the wall which divided her room from that of her parents. She listened; but when no sound could be heard through the wall, slowly, like a deflating tyre, she let herself sink back again into the hollow her body had made in the bed.

It was four o'clock. Eeh! durst she do it? Durst she get up, creep out of the house at this hour? What if she wakened them? Lord, there'd be a set-to if that were to happen. And what would she say? Yes, what would she say? She could never tell them the truth; they would want to lock her in. A little giggle stirred inside her and mounted into a laugh, and she pressed her finger to her lips. Then sitting up she stared towards the glimmer of light at the window. She was surprised to find that she wasn't tired, even though she had danced from eight till twenty to eleven. Had she been only a quarter of an hour alone with him? Had all this been arranged in a quarter of an hour? When they had left the club he hadn't believed it when she said she had to be in by eleven. She had known he thought she was spinning a yarn and just wanted to walk with him a bit longer. He had not tried to kiss her or do any necking, and somehow it was a relief. It was nice not to have to fight when somebody was taking you home, to slap their hands from the front of your dress, to stop their fingers working in your palms. If her dad knew what went on there he would never let her go near the club; although it didn't go on in the club, it was after. And in a way she was glad she had to be in by eleven for she knew she wasn't up to coping with them, as Nancy Leary was with her parents, or Janet Castleton with hers. They could enjoy themselves and go as far as they wanted and hold their own, but she knew she wouldn't be able to. She was always afraid of passing out and leaving herself at the mercy of one or other of them. When she used to go to church, that was before she left school, she would pass out on a Sunday morning, nearly always at the same time, and then her dad put his foot down and wouldn't let her go any more. But that was years ago, years and years and years, when she was fifteen. She laughed to herself again for thinking it was years since she was at school. It was only two years ago.

Well, if she was going to go she had better get up.

Bridget Stevens stood on the bedside mat for a moment, biting at her lip, still undecided; and then with quick jerky movements she was dragging her clothes on, the same clothes that she had taken off last night when she came back from the dance. She hadn't worn a dance frock; she had made that mistake only once, and had sat out all night and not one of the lads had asked her on to the floor. No, her dance dress consisted of a full skirt with a stiff buckram petticoat attached and a V-necked cotton jumper with half sleeves. Her coat lay where she had flung it over the bottom of the bed, and after putting it on she picked up, not the stiletto-heeled, long pointed-toed shoes in which she had danced, but a slipper-like pair that lay under the bed and, carrying these in her hand, she crept to the door.

On the landing, she had to pass her parents' door, and then their Willie's door, which was across the little landing and next to that of the bathroom. When she reached the top of the stairs she opened her mouth wide and silently drew in a long gulp of air. Then cautiously, step by step, she crept down the stairs. She did not attempt to leave the house by the front door opposite, but turned down a narrow hallway into the kitchen, and here, standing by the table, she again opened her mouth wide and gulped air, but not so silently this time. Then, after unbolting the back door she opened it and closed it softly after her. She had forgotten her watch but she heard the clock on St Nicholas's Church striking the quarter: a quarter past four. She would be back at a quarter past six and no one would be any the wiser, for they would still be sleeping; they would sleep till nine o'clock this morning, because it was Sunday. She had never known her mother or father or their Willie rise before the paper-boy came on a Sunday. At nine o'clock on any other morning of the week the house was empty, for they would all have gone to work, her mother included, but Sunday was a day of rest and they took this literally; until nine o'clock anyway.

South Scardyke was the new part of the town and was covered with council houses. The Stevenses had moved here three years ago from East Scardyke when they were pulling the houses down in that quarter. Brid Stevens liked living in South Scardyke, no matter how her dad went on about it, and he did go on about it, proclaiming that her mother had never had to go out to work when they lived at the east side. His money had been sufficient for them all then, but now, even though the four of them were working, it still wasn't sufficient. Brid liked the cleanliness of Cornford Terrace, she liked the cleanliness of the house, she liked having a bathroom, especially when she could get it to herself for an hour or even more. She liked the view from the back bedroom window, their Willie's window, for it looked right across the open ground to the hills, and she knew that if you could have sawn the top off Stockwell Hill you would have had a glimpse of the sea beyond. The sea, the beach and the cliffs were only two miles from South Scardyke, and she was on her way there now. Well, not actually to the sea but to gaze at it from the top of Stockwell Hill.

There was a grass verge along the edge of the pavement, with young trees studding it here and there, and she kept to the verge to dull her steps, in case some light sleeper, hearing footsteps in the street, might look out from behind the curtains. You never could tell, for some people couldn't sleep. She thought this was very strange although she knew it was true: she herself couldn't get enough sleep, yet here she was at a quarter past four on a Sunday morning off to see the dawn and to see the sun rise over the sea from the top of Stockwell Hill. It was daft, wasn't it? She laughed inside and her stomach contracted with excitement. When she reached the end of the street she cut through a gap between the railings of two houses, which brought her to the recreation ground. As she crossed this open space she felt a little fear: this was the place where men waylaid girls at night. But the night was past, the street lamps were out, and the dawn was coming. She felt the light beginning to creep around her.

When she saw the grey outline of Coster Road School looming ahead, she knew she must hurry still more or she'd miss him. Her hurrying came to an abrupt stop when, without seeing anyone, she heard the monotonous tread of steps coming towards her along the road. That was a policeman. Quickly she turned up the side cut by the infants' passage, skirted the railings around the playground, passed the old church of St Nicholas, and then abruptly she was in the country and walking between the high hedges, making for Stockwell Hill. And she became more excited and at the same time frightened than at any time since the alarm had wakened her.

Joe Lloyd had been waiting on Stockwell Hill for more than half an hour now, sitting in the same spot he always occupied. The grass at this spot was worn away and the ground hollowed into a scoop where, years ago, his father had raked the earth away with his bare hands to make him cushy. He hadn't been four years old when his father had first brought him to the top of Stockwell Hill, and early in the morning at that; not at four o'clock, no, not as early as that, but around about seven. And it was something for a youngster to be got out of bed and dressed and walk all this way at that age. It had taken them a solid hour on that first walk, but on their last they made it in twenty-five minutes. The last time his father and he had climbed to this point of contact with God, as his father had once called it, the last time they had come up here was just three days before he was killed. Joe felt no pain now that his father was no longer with him; there was only an emptiness, and this was enclosed within some chamber deep in the private part of his mind. You could not go on feeling and suffering as he had done without something dreadful happening, such as

11

going mad. At one time he had thought he *would* go mad. His mother had said, 'Come out of the pit; that will help.' But he had refused. Among other things, he had inherited certain principles from his father. His father had not been like some pit-men, yelling down the work that sustained him in life. So he had said to his mother, 'No; what was good enough for Dad is good enough for me.' It was strange, he knew, that he should say this, and he knew his mother, too, considered it strange.

It was usually said from the opposite direction: it was usually the father who said, 'What is good enough for me should be good enough for you.' He had nothing against the pit: he could leave the pit the morrow if he wanted to; but he didn't want to, and this was strange, too, because he loved the light, he loved the dawns and sunsets. He did not so much care for the high noons and the blaze of the day, but he liked the shadows when they were pale and fresh in the morning, and he liked them when they were tired at night.

They had sat side by side at this very spot that last day, and his father had talked to him about women. He had spoken to him gently about women. There were other ways to talk about women and Joe knew this already: he had learned a lot in the six months he had been at the pit-head. His father had said quietly, 'I'm not going into details now for I guess you know as much about that side of it as I do; you young 'uns do, the day. Aw, but I think they always did. Woman's the great curiosity shop of life. You wouldn't be a lad if you didn't start groping that way from early on, so we won't go over old ground. But I'd just like to say this, lad, and I'm saying it from experience an' things I've thought out, things that have always been difficult to put into words. Yet now, on a morning like this, they are clear in me mind, and this is one of them, lad. When you go looking for a wife – not just for a lass mind, that's different – when you go lookin' for a wife try to see her as she'll be, say . . . five years on. You'd do better still if you'd try for ten. Now this sounds easy, but it isn't, lad. It's a very difficult thing to do, because if you're looking for a wife you're half in love already and it's gumming up your eyeballs. One tip I'll give you. Never take a lass who says she can't stand a liar, for you can bet your life she doesn't know what the truth is. When they're emphatic about things like that, look out. Look for some gentle streak in her, but don't be misled if she goes all goofy over dogs. By! I've seen some bitches who love dogs.' At this, they had both laughed, they had fallen on their backs and laughed, and when they sat up the tears were running down their cheeks, and his father had pushed him with his thick squat hand and, light with his laughter, he had fallen over again, and there had ended the one and only session of talking about the facts of life.

His father had been a wonderful man. Wonderful was the only word that seemed to fit him. He had been a gentleman ... gentle, the kind that meant tender, yet he could be firm and indomitable about some things. He had been that about not letting his wife go out to work. She had suggested it only once, and Joe remembered his father saying, 'You've got a husband, a bairn and a house, and if these can't keep you goin', lass, then there's something wrong.' It was the quiet way his father had said this that closed the subject for good. His mother had adored his father. Had, was the word; she could obviously adore him no longer.

Joe moved his buttocks in the mould of earth. Only three years had passed and she was thinking of marrying again. He couldn't believe it. The thought still made him sick. A fortnight ago he had first guessed what she was at when he came up on her giving tea to Mr Bishop, the grocer from the high town, and he had wanted to push his fists in Mr Bishop's face. Yet, prior to this, he had always liked the man. After his father went, Mr Bishop had been very good to them. But to have him in the house in his father's place, that was a different kettle of fish. It was because this thought was still troubling him that he had come over from their village of Johnson's Cross into South Scardyke a week gone Saturday night and looked in at the club: he was wanting company, for his mother was no longer his company. If he had sat with her or taken her to the pictures her mind would have been on Mr Bishop. He knew that. So he had made for the club and there had met up again with Sandy Palmer and his lot. Sandy Palmer, Ronnie Fitzsimmons, Clarky Leach, Charlie Talbot, all the lads who had gone to school with him. He was the only one from his class who had taken to the pits and he knew that they thought he was soft on top for doing this.

At school, because of the difference in their height, he had been a little afraid of Sandy Palmer, and now three years later, Sandy had put on another four or five inches. He was six-foot two if he was an inch, whereas he himself had remained practically static. He was five-foot four and a half, and he knew that, like his father before him, he would remain five-foot four and a half. But he was no longer afraid of Sandy Palmer. Yet that wasn't strictly true. He had a certain feeling about Sandy, a feeling that warned him that it was better if they didn't meet, if their paths didn't cross. And perhaps they wouldn't have crossed again if he hadn't seen young Brid Stevens. He remembered her just faintly from their school days, just faintly because she had altered so much. Her eyes were grey and her forehead wide, and her hair was long and thick and swung away from her back as she danced. It was brown when it lay still, but it was gold when it moved. Her thighs were firm and her breasts were high and her face was kind, and she was all of an inch taller than him.

He had been to few dances. When he was fourteen he had gone to the club and one of the women had given some of the lads lessons. She had shown them how to waltz and fox-trot, and he had rather liked her. The club was just beginning then, but soon others came and before long there was nothing but rock-'n'-roll. He had never liked rock-'n'-roll. He didn't like to see girls wriggling like worms on the one spot. He thought they looked like corkscrews that never went through the corks. So when he had asked Brid Stevens to dance and without a word she had stood in front of him and started to wriggle, he had looked at her, then put his arm about her waist and taken her off surprisingly into a clumsy one-step. But in this he had not been able to cover the length of the room before they were pushed and knocked and joggled by the writhing bodies of the jivers. It was jive now, and he had brought ridicule upon them both because he couldn't do it.

During last week he had been to George's Coffee Shop twice and met Brid there. Then, without any dating being done, they had met again last night at the club, and as he looked at her he had tried to visualise what she would look like in five years' time or, say, ten. But he couldn't see her then, he could only see her now, and he knew that he wanted her, wanted her as his father must have wanted his mother, and he said to himself, as his father would have done, 'Now, no nonsense, go slow and careful, and don't frighten her off.' It was odd that he should think this way about her, because she was a regular at the club. She was seventeen and she knew Sandy Palmer and his crowd, and yet he knew that if he put a foot wrong she would be gone. Not out of the club, or South Scardyke, but out of this world that they were both tentatively entering.

At this moment he thought of his father with great tenderness and he got to his feet and looked over the brow of the hill towards the main road, and as he did so he said to himself, 'God, let her come.' And it was as though God had heard him, for instantly he saw a dark shape running along the main road. It disappeared from the sight of his straining eyes for a second behind some shrubs, and when it appeared again he had the urge to run to her as would a little lad who had not yet reached the self-conscious state of knowing he was no longer a lad. He remained still, watching her shape bounding towards him through the gathering light. And then she was standing a short distance from him, so that he had only to put out his hand with his elbow bent to touch her. She was gasping, and he could feel her hot breath on his face; even the warmth of her body came to him, she stood so close. For a moment he reverted to the naturalness of a child and said, 'I thought you weren't coming. Yes, I did.'

'Oh, but I said I would.'

'Aye, I know you did.'

'Well,' – she was still panting – 'I'm here.'

She had moved back from him, and the distance returned the meeting to some normality.

'You're not too soon.'

'No?'

'No, it'll be up any minute.'

'Will it?'

She turned to look towards the sea, but she couldn't make it out. It was as if it wasn't there. But she knew she had only to run down this hill to reach the edge of the tide. Everything was grey and violet. The grey she knew to be the water, the violet the sky. She felt strange, a bit weird, elated. She had the silly desire to laugh.

'Come and sit down. You put a coat on; that was sensible. Look, there's an armchair ready-made.' He pointed to the place where he had been sitting. 'I've warmed it for you.'

When she sat in the hollow she made a sound, half laugh, half an exclamation of amazement at finding the earth so comfortable. She pressed her back into the shape.

'I've never been up so early in me life.'

'No?' He was now sitting on his hunkers by her side, and they were staring at each other full in the face.

'No. It was four o'clock when I got up. The alarm scared me to death. What time did you get up?'

'I've never been to bed.'

'What!' Her chin was drawn into the soft flesh of her neck.

'No; I missed the last bus and I walked.'

'Aw.'

'Aw, nothing. I think I missed it on purpose, just to give meself an excuse. I like walking.'

'But what is it? It must be three . . . four miles from our place to your place.'

'Four and a half. But I didn't go all that way, I came here.'

She screwed round in the earth. 'You mean you've been here all night?'

He nodded, his lips tight and his eyes bright.

'No!'

'There's a bit of a cave down yonder; it's as warm as toast at this time of the year. Me Dad and me spent many a night there.'

'Your Dad?'

'Yes.'

'What did your mother say?'

'Oh, she got used to it; she didn't mind. She used to laugh and say we were no more than a couple of bairns.' His face sobered. 'He's been dead three years now.'

'Your Dad?'

'Yes.'

'I'm sorry. But you still come and sleep out in the cave?'

'Now and again. Not very often, except like last night. It seemed silly to walk the rest of the way home and then come back.'

'Did you think I'd come then?' She was looking towards the sea.

'I hoped you would.' He too was now looking towards the sea; and he exclaimed excitedly, 'Look at the colour. See it spreading along like hot jam slipping over the edge of the table?'

'Yes; yes.' She could see the picture of his description more clearly than the deep blushed horizon, and yet she said, 'What an odd description for the rising sun.'

'Me mother spilt a basin of warm jam she was putting into tarts one day and it ran right along the edge of the kitchen table. I never see that streak of colour unless I see that jam spreading over the whole place.'

She cast her eyes swiftly at him. He was new, nice, delightful somehow. She hadn't known before that she wanted to hear someone talk in this fashion, and yet why else had she gone to the coffee bar on the Monday night following the first Saturday she had seen him? That was only a week ago, a week last night. She must have seen him before when they were at school because he had told her he remembered her, although she couldn't remember him. But from the moment he had asked her to dance and Sandy Palmer and Clarky Leach and the rest had bustled them because they weren't jiving, she had wanted to see him again. She had liked the sound of his voice right from the start. She was sorry that he wasn't as tall as she was, having always told herself she would never go out with a boy who wasn't as tall as herself. But he looked nice somehow, and the way he held himself brought his eyes on a level with her own. Perhaps, she thought, it was the way she did her hair that made her appear taller than him, but she really knew it wasn't. When she was dancing with him his head looked big, big enough to fit a man much taller, and his shoulders looked as though they belonged to a six-footer. He had a wave in his hair that started at his brow and disappeared over the crown of his head. His hair was fair and one part where the wave caught the light looked blond. His eyes were a hazel colour, and they looked kind, soft and gentle. They were different from Sandy Palmer's and he used them differently. He did not keep them looking down the front of your dress or on your mouth until your hands sweated.

'Look,' he said; 'look. It's coming up.'

'Oh, it's bonny. Oh, it is.'

'An' you've never seen it afore?' His voice sounded excited, as if he were displaying to her something magical which he himself had created.

'No.' She was looking to the horizon, now entirely taken up with the blaze of colour erupting over the line of the sea.

As the sun rose with seeming speed she kept exclaiming, 'Oh! Oh!' She had for the moment let the wonder of the dawn supplant the feeling of being alone in the early morning with this boy. She knew that she was experiencing surprise, a beautiful surprise. She had not wanted to see the dawn but she had wanted to be here with this boy in the early morning. But now the dawn was showing her its worth and she became still under the wonder of it. It was so beautiful it was in a way painful, and she wished for a moment that she needn't look at it. As the glow rolled the grey mist back from the sea, almost it seemed to her very feet, she felt filled with an odd choking feeling. She was different somehow . . . she felt clean, washed, like. The dirt of life with which she was daily surrounded, and to which she was forever closing her eyes and stopping her ears, was receding. This light was like a great wet flannel wiping her mind clean.

'I never get used to it, never. It's always new. You know something?'

'No.' Her voice was dreamy.

They were both staring ahead now, their eyes resting gently on the picture before them.

'I think doctors must be daft. They mustn't really be thinking straight.'

'Why? How d'you make that out?'

'Well, just look. If they were to put sick people, especially those sick in their minds, if they were to put them somewhere so they could see the dawn every morning, I can't see but that they wouldn't be cured in next to no time.'

'It might frighten them.'

'The dawn?'

'Yes. Yes, I think it might.' She moved her head slowly while continuing to stare towards the great spreading glow. 'I'm afraid of the moon.'

'You are?'

'Yes, I used to scream at it when I was little. So perhaps this wouldn't do everybody good, 'cos . . . well, it makes you think, like.'

'Yes; yes, it does.' He brought his eyes on to her. He knew he had been right about her, and the intensity of his gaze brought her head round to him.

She was pleased with herself. She was talking, and not about silly things, like Janet and Nancy did in the office. She was pleased to think she knew that the dawn would frighten some people, for she had never realised that she knew this. Yet she had always known there was a different kind of talk from that which she heard at home, and at the office. Nancy and Janet talked of nothing but dress and lads . . . and babies. It was the latter that made her feel the most awkward. She never wanted a baby, never. She had never wanted lads either – well, not until this last day or so – for when she thought of lads she thought of Sandy Palmer or Ronnie Fitzsimmons, and then her thoughts would shift to her mother and father, or her Uncle John, who was Sandy's father and not really her uncle at all. She just called him uncle because they had lived near each other for so long. She said now, 'It would do Sandy Palmer good to come and see this,' and immediately her face lost its light. Why couldn't she leave Sandy Palmer out of this? She hadn't wanted to think of Sandy Palmer.

'Yes, it would that. You live near him, don't you?'

'Yes, three doors away. It's strange, but we used to live three doors away from them in the old town, too, afore we moved.'

'Do you like him?' He asked the question without looking at her and she answered it without looking at him.

'No.'

'He likes you.'

She did not answer, but she looked into the blaze of colour until it dazzled her. She too had thought Sandy Palmer had liked her, had wanted her for his girl. She had never wanted to be his girl and her mother had warned her: 'You keep away from Sandy, don't have any carry on. Mind, I'm tellin' you.' And she had replied, 'What! me and Sandy Palmer? I don't want Sandy Palmer . . . Him!' only for her mother to say,

24

'All right, but mind, I'm tellin' you,' whatever she was implying by that . . . mother's warning.

Sandy never came to the house, never called for her, but whenever she was at the club he was there and he would walk back with her, even when she left early. She had tried to push him off: she cheeked him, snapped at him, tried ridicule, but it was no good. If she went home with Nancy Leary he would walk behind them, talking at them. Sometimes he would be alone, and sometimes there would be Ronnie Fitzsimmons or Charlie Talbot with him. Charlie Talbot lived on the other side of the Palmers and was nothing but a little toad. He went around with Sandy Palmer because he was a sucker-up and wanted to be in with the motor-bike crowd. But quite abruptly, about three weeks ago, Sandy Palmer had let her go home alone. He had been in the club all one evening and never once asked her to dance, hadn't even spoken to her. But he had kept looking at her in an odd kind of way. If she hadn't known him she would have called it a frightened way, but she did not think of fear and Sandy Palmer together, for he was afraid of nothing and no-one. Perhaps it was just coincidence that the time he stopped speaking to her should be the day after her mother and dad had had a terrible row, and yet it wasn't so odd, because the Palmer family and hers were connected with a link that was a source of misery to her. No matter what joy she felt, it was impregnated with this misery; the connection between the Palmers and themselves. Life was horrible, dirty, dirty . . .

'Don't let it make you look so sad.'

'What? What! Oh no. No, I'm not sad. It's bonny. It's too bonny to make you sad. It's the bonniest dawn I've ever seen.' She laughed. 'That's silly, as it's the only one I've ever seen. But it won't be the last.' Her eyes were bright again, looking straight into his. 'I can hardly see your face; it's the colours, they've almost blinded me.'

'You shouldn't stare like that, you should keep blinking and not look at the sun directly. Look away to the side. You were staring as if you were looking beyond it, from where it comes.'

'From where it comes?' A soft smile touched her lips. 'You say the funniest things. I suppose it comes up from Australia.'

Now he laughed. 'It doesn't come up from anywhere. It's us that comes up. It's always there. You know I worried about it when I first learned it was us who did the moving.'

'Why did you worry?'

'Oh, well, when you accept a thing you don't think about it, but when you look at a thing and know that you're not seeing what you're looking at, or what you're looking at isn't really there, if you know what I mean, well then, one thing leads to another and then you start asking questions. It worries me a bit even now when I know I'm standing on the crust of the earth and it's going round. I know now that it's gravitation that keeps me put, but what is gravitation? That worried me for a long time. I don't even know the answer yet.' He laughed self-consciously.

She said, 'Do you write poetry?'

'What me? Poetry? No. What gave you that idea?'

'They said you would.'

'Who?'

'They: Nancy Leary and Janet Castleton, Clarky and . . .' there it was again, the name, 'Sandy Palmer.'

'Sandy Palmer? Was he talking about me?'

'They were all talking around the table at George's. They were talking about the beats in London and the poetry sessions. They said it was cranky. And then they were asking who knew any poetry and they said that the only ones around the club who would be able to spout poetry were Leslie Baker and you.'

'Sandy Palmer said that?'

'Yes, and the others.'

'Well, I can't write poetry; I don't even like it. I don't write at all and I don't want to. Too many people are writing things they know nothing about. You've just got to pick up magazines or books. Half of them write about places they've never been to . . . they get it all from the library. I've seen them sittin' there. One of the journalists from the paper, the one that writes

27

under the name of "Adventurer", he's never out of the reference library.'

'No?'

'No. And I've never written poetry or anything else.'

He sounded vehement all of a sudden and she wondered why. Perhaps because he wanted to write and couldn't. Yet he sounded to her clever enough to write.

Joe was pleased that she thought he could write, poetry or anything else, but at the same time he was vexed that the subject had been brought up solely because he couldn't do what Sandy Palmer and the rest gave him credit for; write poetry, or anything else. He wasn't really telling the truth when he said he didn't write anything. He *had* tried his hand at it, again and again. His head was full of things he wanted to write, but his spelling was awful, his style was worse, and when he attempted it he couldn't get the stuff on to the paper for thinking how awful his spelling was. He was more concerned about his spelling than his writing, for he spelt phonetically and he knew now that was something to be ashamed of. He wished he had paid more attention at school, he wished he could have another chance, and yet he knew if he could have another chance it would be the same all over again. He wasn't one who could learn from books or reading, he could only learn by looking and listening. He learned more from listening to a chap talking about a subject on the radio than he had ever done by reading books on the subject. And again, if the subject was to do with nature, he learned more by using his eyes on a long walk than listening to all the authorities on the radio. He wished he could write, he wished he could. But he'd never be able to. The things in his head would only come out through talking, and there were few people he had met to whom he really wanted to talk. But there were some, and Brid here was one of them. He felt the heat of happiness pass over him at the thought. It was wonderful that he had found a girl at last that he could talk to, that he wanted to talk to, and one who wanted to listen to him. He was nineteen and he had begun to give up hope that he would ever find a girl he could talk to, just sit like this and talk to. But he mustn't let her think he was stuffy and that all he could do was talk. He said quickly, 'You like to dance?'

'Yes. Yes, I love it.' The admission was given in a tone of apology.

'You're a good dancer.'

'You think so?'

'The best at the club, I'd say.'

'Oh no, I'm not; there are many better than me. But I like it.'

'I'm no good at this jive stuff, that's why I don't do it.' He was making amends for his attitude on the dance floor the previous evening when yet once again he refused to stand like a jolting puppet while she dizzied and whirled in front of him. He had thought privately that those that wanted to have St Vitus's dance could have it, but he wasn't going to. And again, that the girls looked like cock birds out to attract the hens. The positions had been reversed and it wasn't nice. Modern times or no modern times, man should do what preening there was to be done.

'I don't mind what I dance so long as I dance.'

They remained silent now as they looked at each other, and then they laughed and looked towards the sun again.

'See there! Isn't that wonderful? See there! That line of rocks, they're all purple. You would think they were lit up by headlights, wouldn't you?' He pointed away to the far right towards where the land sloped more gently to beach level.

She nodded, then said, 'But they say there're quicksands there.'

'Maybe; but people don't swim over there; the rocks here are a protection, but yon side of them is deeper and dangerous. This side, I've bathed for years.'

'You have?'

'Yes.'

'But it's got a warning up that bathing is forbidden, that it's dangerous.'

'Yes, it would be if you didn't know what you were

at. Well look, the tide's out now and there's still some water this side of the rocks, deep enough to swim in and it's as safe as houses.'

'Have you ever been beyond?'

'No; I wouldn't want to. It's deeper, and the undercurrent is strong. I went in once, and by! it didn't half frighten me. That was a year or two ago. But you needn't go as far as the rocks, even. You can swim all you want just off the sand. And there's this about it, you don't get the crowds here. Many locals come. That notice is just for the holidaymakers who don't know what they're at. This afternoon you won't be able to put a pin on this hill if it's fine; everybody'll be picnicking. And on the beach an' all.' He said again quickly, ahead of her, as if he were leading the way through passages of thought, 'I never want to leave this place.'

'You mean here?' She flapped her hand towards the ground.

'No . . . Yes, but not just this spot. The coastline. Oh, the coastline's grand up here. Look at it. Where will you see a grander sight than that?'

She followed his moving arm. She hadn't thought about it before. In all the years she had lived so near to the sea she had scarcely paid it any attention. She had taken the train into Morpeth every morning for over two years now and her nights seemed to have been taken up with hurrying home and getting the tea ready for her mother and dad coming in from work. They got in a quarter-past six, but the tea and washing up were never over before half-past seven. Then they would look at the telly. Her father never left her mother on her own at night, except when her Uncle John called in, and if that happened he and her dad went along to the club.

On such occasions, when they were left alone together, her mother would talk to her. She was different altogether when they were alone. She would put her arm round her waist and pull her up beside her on the couch and they would laugh about things. She was jolly at heart, was her mother, and she would often say to her, 'Come on, come on; don't look so sad. Prepare to enjoy yourself;' and she would laugh and quote the advert, which said, 'Prepare to be a beautiful lady'. But sometimes, even right in the middle of her laughter, she would suddenly turn serious, almost fierce, and say things like, 'Enjoy yourself; you're only young once. My God! you are. But not with Sandy Palmer, mind;' and her eyes would widen as she gave this apparent warning. 'Keep clear of Sandy Palmer, he's no good for you.'

Then, later in the evening, even though there might be a serial or some other interesting programme on the television, her mother would assuredly hear the back gate click and then the dual footsteps on the cement path, and she would watch her mother lean her head against the back of the couch and laugh, but quietly to herself. Then she would close her eyes, and when the two men entered the room she would always say the same thing; without turning her head to look at them she would say, 'We . . . ell!' Just like that. 'We . . . ell!'

And so in the evenings, even in the summer, she had never gone for walks by the shore. Once or twice on a Sunday afternoon she had gone out with Janet and got as far even as this point, but they had never descended the hill to the shore. For one thing it would have spoiled their shoes, and for another it had always looked so grim and forbidding to her. But now she wondered why she had ever thought that. It was beautiful, made beautiful by the dawn, this bonny dawn. Oh, it was a bonny dawn. Even if she hadn't been here with Joe Lloyd she imagined she would still have thought it was a bonny dawn, she couldn't help but.

'Look, every place is alight now.' His roving gaze finished on her and he repeated, 'Every place.' For her face was warm and rosy as if she had just got out of a hot bath, and her eyes were reflecting the colours of the morning. He could see the streaks of dawn light going down into them. And yet they were all grey, a bright clear grey . . . and wise. Her mouth was open, just enough to show two large white front teeth, and her lips were like painted joy as they spread when she exclaimed with her finger pointing, 'Look! there's a boat, a little boat. It must have been there all night. Fishing?'

'Oh yes; fishing.'

'It looks yellow and dark blue to me. What colour does it look to you?'

He laughed: 'Yellow and dark blue,' although he couldn't see it.

She said again 'Oh!' and her hands hugged at her knees. It was as if she had never before seen a fishing boat or imagined that anyone could stay out in a boat all night; and this was silly, because their Willie often went fishing at night. He went with Harry Palmer. They were both saving up to buy a boat, rather than a car. They both said they'd had enough of cars, driving their lorries. Their Willie and Harry Palmer had been pals since they were at school. In this, they merely followed the pattern of their fathers, because her father and her Uncle John had been pals when they were young, too, and they still were. At this point in her thinking, her head jerked and her mind went back to her brother Willie, and she thought, It's funny, he's never had a girl. Harry Palmer never bothered with girls, either. He used to, her mother said, until he was about twenty, and then he and Willie started to go fishing. They both worked for the same contractor and drove the long-distance lorries, sometimes as far as London and back. They nearly always managed to go on the same consignment. But when they didn't manage it, their Willie mooned about the house and didn't even go near the boat. Over the years, the boat had become as familiar as her own bike and yet she had never seen it. They hired it from Crosby's up at the Bay, and she understood they always managed to get the same one. But when they got their own they would likely take her out in it. She rather liked their Willie and would have liked to be closer to him, to talk to him, but she had the feeling that he always pushed her off, evaded her. Yet when there were any rows in the house he supported her.

As she looked at the boat bobbing up and down in her line of sight she visualised herself lying in bed, her head pressed into the pillow and her hands over her ears to shut out the murmur of her father's voice from the next room. Her flesh crept when her father talked in that low entreating tone, but there was the night when he had screamed at her mother, and then she had heard Willie's door open and his voice crying across the empty landing towards his parents' room: 'Give over! you two, will you? Don't you know there's somebody next door?'

She knew that Willie hadn't been referring to the Pratts, but to her. She remembered his last words before he went back into his room and banged the door, 'God Almighty! at your age.' It was then she heard her father bounce out of bed. He seemed to jump from the bed on to the landing, so quickly came his voice yelling to his son: 'My age! Who the hell do you think I am? Methuselah?' Her father had been forty-five at that time, and she fourteen. Then she thought she heard him mutter, 'The unnatural bugger.'

In other ways, too, Willie had tried to protect her against her father, and she had been puzzled up until recently by the fact that she should need this protection, but she knew she did. She was afraid of her father, yet she knew she could have loved him if he had let her. But he too pushed her off, much more so than Willie did. Her mother didn't push her off, her mother drew her close, yet she had known right from a child that her mother was the cause of the trouble in the house. This on the face of it was strange, for her mother was bonny and laughing, and quite kind. Perhaps she laughed too much really, but it was often at herself. She laughed the day she got her hair bleached. It had been a mousey brown and was going grey, and she had had it bleached. Willie had laughed and she had laughed with him, but her father had nearly gone mad.

Her eyes still on the boat, she took a great gulp of air into her lungs and as she let it out she muttered on the fringe of audibility, 'Oh, if we only didn't live near the Palmers.'

'What d'you say?'

'Oh, nothing. Well, I was just looking at the boat. My brother goes fishing.'

'I didn't know you had a brother; I thought you were the only one.'

'No, he's much older than me, he's twenty-six. He and Harry Palmer go out and sometimes stay out all night, fishing. He's Sandy's brother.' She turned her head towards him now and her face was serious. 'He's not a bit like Sandy, he's nice. Harry's a year older than our Willie. Everybody says they're like twins, they're always together.'

'It's nice to have a pal like that. I've got a pal; he's what you call my marrer.' He laughed as he gave her this information. 'He's two years older than me; he had his twenty-first birthday last week. By! there was a do. He'll just be coming up now.' He lifted his eyes towards the sky as if he were with his friend and the cage had just stopped and they were taking their first fill of light. 'We've been on different shifts for the last three weeks; it's the cut of the draw.'

'Would he have been with you all night if you had been on the same shift?'

'Not him.' Again he laughed. 'He thinks I'm up the pole. But we go to cricket together, and in the winter I always watch him play football. He's a grand footballer; he should have been a professional. Ossie, short for Oswald. He hates his name.' Joe smiled sympathetically. 'And I don't blame him.'

She looked towards the beach. The last lap of the tide had gone completely down now and licked lazily at the sand. She could see it leaving a line of bubbles, shining, rainbow-hued bubbles. The whole stretch of coastline looked like one great mouth and the tide like a tongue, as though it were the mouth of a happy dog with saliva dripping from it. But the picture was not translated into thought in her mind – her thoughts were taken up with Ossie. She did not like the sound of this Ossie. She felt that if they had been on the same shift Joe wouldn't have been here, nor would he have come to the club in the first place. He had come down there because he was at a loose end. She felt suddenly frightened at the fact of so much depending on so little. If Joe hadn't been at a loose end, if his pal hadn't been on the other shift, if . . . if. A sense of insecurity enveloped her. She was here just by chance, just because Joe had found himself at a loose end. She was being forced to the fringe of the deep fundamental fact that life itself was but a chance thing. She said quickly, 'Eeh! I'll have to be getting back now,' and before he could look at her she had swung herself up in an easy movement that spoke of youth. In a second, he was standing in front of her.

'Have you minded comin'?'

'No; oh no. I've loved it. I've never seen anything like it in me life.'

'Will you come again?'

'Yes, yes.'

'Do you swim?'

'Yes. Oh, yes, I can swim.'

'Are you doing anything this afternoon?'

'No. No, I'm not.' They were looking at each other, unblinking.

'Will we go swimming over there?' He did not take his eyes from her but motioned towards the bay.

'Yes. Yes, if you like.'

'The tide should be right just about two.'

'Oh, I don't think I could manage it at that time. You see there's Sunday dinner and . . .'

'Oh, I know. Me mother's the same; you've got to have the lot on Sunday. I've always thought that's a bit funny. Me dad used to think it funny an' all. He used to say that they could stew the guts out of bones all the week and half starve, but on the Sunday they had the lot. Six veg, some of them had. Aye, you wouldn't believe it. Some in our street are still like that. But not me mother. Oh no; me mother's a grand cook.'

She was staring at him; she loved to hear him talk. There was a lilt to his voice, a sort of hidden laughter, and yet it sounded sad. She thought it was what could be called a deep rich voice. It seemed bigger than his whole body; like his head and shoulders, it didn't seem to belong to the rest of him. She saw him look away towards the road where she thought she heard a car passing, but she didn't take her eyes off his face. The sun was playing on his hair, and now it looked all silver.

Joe had glanced towards the road to the lorry. It was too far away to make out whose lorry it was, but his attention had been drawn to it when he'd heard it stopping. If it had been racing past down the road it would have been gone in a flash from his view. But it must have been going slowly for a while. As he looked at it he could make out the shape of the driver in the cab. It actually stopped only for a second and went off again, and he brought his gaze and thoughts back to her. She was pretty. And not just pretty . . . there was something about her that required a name. He would have to think. It wasn't beautiful. No, she wasn't beautiful, not as girls are beautiful. Was it exquisite? Oh no; that meant something beyond beauty. No, it wasn't exquisite. Homely? No, man, no, he said to himself; that was the other extreme. And yet she could be. Yes, she could be homely. He tried to see her in five, ten, fifteen years' time, but he couldn't. He could only see her now, and with sudden contradiction of his previous summing up, he thought: Yes, she is, she is beautiful.

'Well, I'd better be going. I want to get back before six.'

'You'll make it. I'll come part of the way.'

'No, no.' For some reason she didn't want him to walk back with her. She wanted to keep the feeling of him in the dawn; the morning was coming up rapidly now and she didn't want him to come into the morning.

He was all light as he was now. She did not want him to become part of the grey tone of the morning . . . all mornings.

'All right,' he said. 'But look.' He turned and pointed. 'I'll be along there. Don't mind what time you can come, the day's me own. Right at the end where the cliff levels out; just above that there's a bit of woodland. It's lovely up there. I'll show you. The blackberry blossom is comin' thick. It's a week since I saw it, so it should be like snow now.'

She had to tear herself away from his talking, for she found that she was waiting, waiting for him to say something unusual, strange, nice.

'All right, bye-bye then.'

Two

S HE WASN'T FOREWARNED IN ANY WAY. THE curtains in the front room were still drawn across the window, there was no life outside the house, none in the street, none in the town as yet, except for the milkman's electric cart that had joggled past her as she came round by the school. She had so forgotten the unusualness of her morning jaunt that she did not prepare herself for secrecy until she had taken half a dozen steps up the path; and then she lifted her heels from the ground and made her way to the back door on tip-toe.

There was a smile on her face as she stealthily turned the lock back, and then her loud cry of 'Eeh! Oh!' swept it away as her eyebrows lifted the whole skin of her face in shocked, frightened surprise. There sat her mother at the small kitchen table: she had her hands joined tightly together and they looked a dirty grey in contrast with the pale pink plastic covered top of the table. She was wearing a red dressing gown and it was open in a V down between her breasts. She was staring at Brid and she made no move from the table.

Her father was standing near the sink. He was wearing only his trousers; the sparse hair at the back of his head was standing up as it did when he was agitated, for when he was agitated he would run his fingers through it. The hair on his chest was thicker than that on his head, and it was black and curly. He too stared at her, his mouth open as if it were jammed wide.

Willie, in a pair of mauve coloured pyjamas, was standing near the door. He looked big, even massive in his night attire and more attractive than he did during the day. His round face was pink-hued and sleep was still in his eyes, but his face was tight as if he was holding back an outburst. Next to him stood Harry Palmer. Harry was still in his working clothes; the three-quarter length jacket that he wore on long journeys remained buttoned up to his neck, although the morning was already warm. He was the only one not staring at Brid; he had his cap in his hands and his heavy masculine face was bent towards it.

'Well?' It was her mother speaking, but it was a

different 'well' from that with which she greeted the men: there was no light scorn in it; her anger left no room for that. 'What have you been up to?'

Brid cast her eyes swiftly from one to the other, her mouth at the same time half open in protest. She was indignant at the implication in the 'Well?' and the attack in the last words. 'Why, Mother, I've—'

'You leave this to me.' It was her father speaking. He was moving from the sink towards her. 'Where've you been?'

Her head swung two or three times backwards and forwards in the automatic movement of a doll before she exclaimed, 'I've just been along—' her hand went out now and wagged towards the kitchen window, and she swallowed and finished, 'along the top of the cliff.'

Her father was standing in front of her, glaring at her as if he hated her. Ever since she was a child she had had the impression that he didn't like her. She had once said this to her mother and her mother had laughed and said, 'Don't be silly; your dad thinks the world of you.'

'Who was the fella?' he now demanded.

'You . . . you wouldn't know him, he's not from here. He's . . . he's . . .'

'Who was he?'

'His name is Joe Lloyd.'

'Joe Lloyd?'

'He . . . he lives over in Johnson's Cross.'

'Is he going to marry you?'

'Marry me?' Her voice was crawling up the back of her throat now. 'Marry me?' There was a frightened choking sensation in her chest and it jolted into her mouth and made her cough as her father exclaimed, 'I said, marry you, you dirty little bitch, you!'

'I've done nothing, nothing I tell you. I only went out—'

'We know what you did.' He was wagging his hand within an inch of her face, so close that she had to bend backwards away from him. 'You came in from the dance at eleven. Oh aye, I heard you, you dirty little sod, you. And then you slipped out, didn't you, when we were all snug asleep, an' he was waiting for you outside?'

'No, he wasn't. He wasn't . . . Mother –' she looked past her father and appealed to her mother; and her mother staring back at her, pityingly now, said, 'It's no good, Brid; Harry saw you.'

'But he couldn't have; I didn't do anything. We didn't do anything. We were only sitting on the top of Stockwell Hill. We went to see the dawn.'

'My God! . . . be quiet, girl!' The words were groaned out. Her mother was looking at her joined hands again.

'I tell you we were. I don't care what you think you saw, Harry Palmer, that's all we were doing.' There

46

were tears in her voice now, an indignant yet pitiful sound, as she glared at Harry Palmer.

Harry Palmer bowed his head again. He wished he was in hell, this minute. He had never meant it to take this turn. His headlights had picked out the shape of entwined couples at intervals during the night, some in cars too clagged together at that time in the morning to be married. One couple, so young they looked like lost children, were asleep near a rick. It had just got light when he saw that pair. Not long after that, he had been so startled that he had nearly swerved off the road, when, with the sun on her face and her head back, he had seen young Brid standing close to a fella and gazing at him as if she were entranced. It had given him a gliff. What could he do? By the time he had reached the depot he was thinking that he must have been seeing things. Yet he had scampered home, gone straight into the Stevenses' garden and lifted the prop and tapped on Willie's window. This was the usual signal for getting him up without disturbing the house. He had beckoned him down and told him what he had seen. Willie had dived upstairs and, sure enough, he had returned to say her bed was empty. What could he do but rouse his parents? He was sorry, sorry to the heart that he had to be the one to give her away for, in spite of everything, she was a decent kid, was Brid . . . At least he had always thought so.

'You're a liar, Harry Palmer, whatever you say.

It's lies, lies. We were just looking at the sun coming up.'

'Shut your silly trap.' Her father's hand was raised, the back towards her face ready to skelp it when her mother cried, harshly now, 'We'll have none of that! You leave her be.'

Her voice indicated that she was about to take charge of the household once more. But Tom Stevens was not taking any of that this morning. His face blazing with anger, he turned on her: 'Leave her be, eh? Leave her be? Aye, you can say that. There's been too many in this house let be, that's the trouble. Leave her be? Aye, I'll leave her be after I've stripped the flesh off her bones. She's one I'll cure of her whoring.'

'Shut your mouth! you'll have the place raised.' Alice Stevens's voice was low as if it were coming from deep in her bowels. She and her husband were facing each other as if they were alone in the kitchen, enacting one of their usual rows. Then quite abruptly she turned to Harry Palmer and said quietly, 'Thanks for coming, Harry.'

It was a dismissal, and the young man shrugged his body from one side to the other heavily before moving away, and as he reached the door he looked at Brid for a second with a shame-faced look and muttered something below his breath, which sounded like, 'Sorry it had to be me, Brid. Sorry.'

When the door closed on Harry, Brid, her eyes

stretched, her mouth trembling, watched her father glare at it and speak to it, saying, 'Aye, that'll give them something to chew over. We'll have the big fella along here in next to no time wanting the facts. And why not, eh? Why not?' He had, as it were, thrown these last words at his wife, and she said again deeply, 'Shut your mouth!'

Brid felt sick in her stomach. Her father had referred to his life-long friend and pal, the man she called her Uncle John, as if he were a stranger, or at best a neighbour whom he didn't like. He had referred to him as 'the big fella' and he had put hate into the name.

She went to move quietly across the room when her father's arm shot out and barred her way. 'No, you don't! We'll get to the bottom of this or I'll bloody well know the reason why.'

'There's nothing to get to the bottom of, I've told you.' Her head bounced at him, and he stormed on her now: 'Nothing to get to the bottom of?' he cried. 'You're another one who can treat it lightly. It comes of practice, eh? How many times have you done this afore? You little tart, you! Sneaked out on a Saturday night, eh? Come on, out with it.' He had gripped her shoulders and was pulling her back towards the table, when Willie, who so far hadn't spoken, said quietly, 'Enough of that. You can get to the bottom of it without any rough play.'

'You an' all stay out of this,' his father quickly

warned him. Then changing his tone as if he were continuing a reasonable conversation, he said, 'You know what I'm gettin' at. You know what it's all about, don't you? so leave me to deal with this.'

'You're not the one to deal with it; you're too prejudiced.'

'Prejudiced!' Tom Stevens's tone had changed again, and he glared at his son as he cried, 'You call me prejudiced after what I've had to put up with; another man would have—'

'Yes, another man would have . . . another man would have . . .' Her mother's lips were curling right back from her top teeth, and the gesture exposed this man for what his wife and son and herself knew him to be: a man who was all talk. A fearful man. Fearful in the sense that he dreaded losing the one person who was nothing to him now but a form of torture, but without whom he couldn't hope to live.

Brid felt her father's exposure like a deep cut from broken glass. She closed her eyes against it. Then the next moment they were flung wide as, stung into retaliation, he cried, 'You've gone too far. I've told you you would go too far. I'll throw her out, I'll throw her along the road where she belongs, but, and bloody damn you! not afore I've left me mark on her.'

It happened so quickly that she could only instinctively shield her face against him. Pinto's lead always hung on the nail to the side of the kitchen door. It was half leather and half chain and it was the chain that caught her shoulder and lifted her screaming from the ground. She was cowering over the table, her face buried in her arms, as the struggle went on behind her. When her mother's arms came above her and lifted her, the room was quiet. She knew that her father and Willie were standing somewhere near, she could hear their deep shuddering breaths, but she did not look at them. Her mother led her towards the door into the hallway, and there she drew her to a momentary halt, and her sagging breasts were dragged upwards as she turned to look back at her husband. And when she spoke, her words were guttural and deep with threat: 'My God! I'll take it out of you for this, you see if I don't!'

There was a deep moan engulfing Brid's body. It was from a variety of pains. She was holding her hand over the place where the physical pain was most keen, the thick part of her neck at the top of her shoulder where the end of the chain had caught her; there was the pain from her mind where the thoughts, breaking the skin of years, were forcing their way through into the daylight; there was the pain of her spirit, humiliated, brought low, made to feel guilty; and there was the pain which came from she knew not where, the pain of the severed blood-tie. Above all the other pains, this was the worst. It had to do with her father's dislike of her, and her Uncle John's liking of her.

Her father had put into words that which for years now she had dreaded to hear. Her father had never done anything in the whole of her life to make her like him, and he had just struck her. He had, she knew, always wanted to strike her, and now he had done it. Yet still she could not hate him, she could not even actively dislike him, because she still wished he *was* her father, her real father. She didn't want her Uncle John for a father, because her mother wasn't married to her Uncle John, she was married to Tom Stevens, the man who *should* be her father.

Her mother was gently taking off her dress; her hands were soft and warm. She should turn to her and fling herself on her gaping bosom and get the sympathy that she knew was waiting for her, but she didn't. If there was anybody she disliked at this moment it was her mother. Yet her mother had always been kind to her. Her mother was kind to everybody with the exception of her father. She was known as a good sort, her mother was. An intruding thought told Brid that life would have been different had her mother distributed her kindness a little more evenly, then her father wouldn't have been so bad. She still thought of the man downstairs as her father. She would always think of him as her father. Life would have been happy, even joyous, had her mother been faithful to him, for her father could have been a nice man. He still could be a nice man, and it all depended on her mother. But her mother would never give him again what would make him into a nice man. Time had done too much to them.

As her mother pressed her gently into the pillow she felt in an odd way that her father had not really hit her, he had hit her mother.

'Lie still. I'll go and get some of me cold cream and rub it on. The skin isn't broken, but you're likely to have a mark there. But never you mind, I'll take it out of the sod for this. I'll make the bugger squirm.'

'Mother.'

'Yes?'

'Don't do anything. He didn't mean it; I know he didn't mean it.'

'He meant it all right. He's a vindictive sod, always has been. Well, you're old enough now; we'll have to have a talk, and soon.'

Although the movement was painful Brid turned her entire body away from her mother and stared at the wall.

Looking down at her daughter, Alice Stevens sighed. Well, she had to start some time, she supposed, but she'd had the idea that Brid was a bit different, that she'd wait until she married. She herself had known all about it long afore she married Tom Stevens. And it was just as well she got her fun in first, for it would have been a poor lookout after. Why in the name of God had she to go and pick a fellow like Tom?

One-woman man all right, he was. She could have stood it if he'd gone off the rails, even before she herself had started. But God almighty! this till death us do part business got on her tripe. And what had he expected her to do, with him away in the services? Do tattin'? It was himself who had said to John 'Look after her,' and John had looked after her . . . and how! And he would have been looking after her still were it not for Olive. Duty, be damned! Why the hell must he keep yarping on about Olive and his duty. He should have left her and come away when Brid was born.

Silently she turned her head towards her daughter's stiff, still form. Then contracting the muscles of her stomach, she ground out under her breath, 'To hell!' then left the room.

Crossing the landing, she almost kicked open her bedroom door; but, on finding the room empty, she closed it quietly behind her and began to dress. She put on a sleeveless summer frock that displayed her thick fleshy arms. The flesh was in hard nodules like the ridges you see on wet sand. It was a sign of ageing flesh. Yet time that was ravishing her skin was having no effect on the burning, desiring life within her. She was so made that she would keep her vitality until her dying day, however far away that was. The life urge seemed to renew itself daily in her, churning up her whole body and troubling her. Yet it did not show in her movements, which were slow.

She left the bedroom, only to come face to face with Willie. He blocked her way to the stairs. Standing head and shoulders above her, he said, 'If this goes on I'm moving.'

'Now don't you start!'

'Well, it's getting past it. An' people talkin'.'

At this she deliberately widened her eyes and mouth at him in mock surprise, and then she laughed. 'Talkin', you say? People are talkin'? That's good, that is.'

She felt a sense of victory as she watched the hot colour sweep upwards over his face, and when he side-stepped from her and made for his room she turned and said to his back, 'You want to think afore you speak, me lad . . . Talkin'.'

She did not immediately descend the stairs but stood looking down them, saying to herself, 'Talkin'. Talkin'. That's good, that is.' And as she stood there a sadness crept over her, and she turned her head slowly and looked back towards her son's door. Why had this thing that was full and flush in her . . . yes, and in his father an' all, give him his due, to take a twist like it had done in their son . . . ? Oh God, life was hell.

In the kitchen, Tom was sitting at the table, his head resting on his hands. He did not move when she came in and she did not speak to him, but she clashed and banged around him as she set about getting the breakfast ready, and when, putting a tray on the table, she deliberately struck viciously at his elbows, he raised his head and said quietly, 'One of these days I'll forget meself and do you in.'

'Huh!' she almost spat. 'I'll be waitin' for you!'

Tom looked at her for some minutes before he pulled himself up from the table. His eyes were still on her as he hitched his trousers up and moved out of the room. Slowly he mounted the stairs, and as he crossed the landing his eyes flicked towards Brid's door, but he did not stop. When he entered the bedroom he sat down on the side of the tumbled bed and, lifting one hand, he covered his face. After a few moments he lowered his hand and placed his thumb across his mouth and bit hard on it. He would . . . he would. One of these times he would forget himself and go for her, and he would only have to start and he wouldn't be able to stop, he knew he wouldn't. Funny, but he had never hit her. He had been near it a hundred times, but he just couldn't, somehow. And she knew it, blast her. But the other one – he never thought of her as Brid – he felt he wanted to belt her till the blood ran, and he would. She wouldn't go the same road as her mother, he'd see to that. His teeth eased off his thumb and now he flicked them with his nail. What would Palmer's reaction be to the latest? He would have liked to see his face when Harry gave him the news. It would have been a sort of payment for all he had endured. Why had he put up with it all these years? Keeping pals with him knowing what he knew . . . Why? He shook his head.

It was getting that way that he couldn't let him out of his sight in case Alice and he got together. And they laughed at him, at least she did, when his shift worked out and he was on late turn every three weeks . . . If he could only catch them at it. He put his elbow on the bed rail and lowered his head and rested it on his hand. It was as if he were turning from the sight of himself, his fear, his cowardice. He could have caught them time and again but that would have meant facing up to the situation, and he couldn't. Not now, for it had gone on too long. He couldn't live without Alice. Rather she should torture him than leave him. Of a sudden he had the horrifying sensation that he was going to cry. It brought him up on to his feet, and grabbing from here and there, he got into his clothes.

'There, come on, sit up and have this. I've brought me cup up so's I can have one with you. There . . . there now. Eat that up while it's hot: the bacon's nice and crisp, just as you like it.' Alice put the tray on Brid's knees.

'I couldn't eat anything.'

'Don't be silly, get it into you. It isn't the end of the world.'

Brid watched her mother pull a chair up to the foot of the bed and sit down. Through the window at her back the sun shone on her hair, giving to it the appearance of a large halo.

'I couldn't eat anything, I couldn't.'

'Are you sure?'

'Yes.'

'Well, have that bit of toast then and a cup of tea
. . . Hand me the plate; there's no use in wasting it;
it's no good when it's cold.'

Brid watched her mother. She was eating the bacon
as if she were enjoying it, as if nothing had happened.
And then she contradicted this by wiping her mouth
on the pad of her thumb and saying quickly, 'Well
now, let's get this straightened out. Come on, tell me
all about it.'

Brid looked down into the cup she was holding
between her hands. 'There's nothing to tell, nothing
to straighten out. Nothing . . . Nothing,' and she laid
deep quiet emphasis on the last two words.

'Well now' – her mother's tone was patient, and
yet had a hopeless ring about it – 'you don't stay out
all night and have nothing to tell. You know me; I
wasn't born yesterday, girl. And look, I'm not goin'
to get mad at you. I understand, good God! don't I?
Let's face up to things: you're part of me, you're the
same inside as I am, and I know how I am, so don't
be afraid to speak.'

'I tell you, Mother—'

'All right, all right; you were out all night and
nothing happened. Well, then, tell me why you stayed
out all night with him.'

'I didn't. I tell you I didn't; I never left this room until four o'clock.'

'Why four o'clock?'

Brid bowed her head. How could she tell this woman who suggested that her flesh craved the same satisfactions as her own, who knew no other desires, how could she say to her, I went to see the dawn come up? But she would have to, she could only tell the truth. She was looking into her cup again when she said, 'I went to see the dawn come up.'

'Aw, lass.' Her mother's voice sounded more hopeless now, and when it added the usual 'Well!' the word, translating itself to Brid, said, Aw, stop it for God's sake. Come off it. Come clean. What does it matter, anyway? You'll sleep with somebody sooner or later, so come on, let's have it.

'Mother.' The room became quiet for a moment as their eyes held. 'I came in at five past eleven last night. I put me alarm on and I got up at four o'clock this morning because I had promised him I would go and see the dawn from the top of Stockwell Hill . . . And I went . . . And that's all that happened. Harry couldn't have seen anything for nothing happened. I'm tellin' you, Mother. Well, look at the alarm . . . you can see it's set for four.' Her words had ended on a run.

Her mother did not look at the alarm but said, 'Did you see him . . . Harry?'

'No.'

'What were you doin'?'

'Just sitting looking at the colours on the sea.'

Brid watched her mother's eyes drop away, and her teeth drew her lower lip tightly into her mouth as she listened to her saying, 'Harry said he passed numbers of them along the road on his journey. It was a warm night; I suppose that was it. But you were just sittin'?' Her eyes lifted again, and Brid said slowly and quietly, 'Yes, we were just sittin'.'

'And it was dark when you left the house?'

'Yes.'

'Was it dark when you got there?'

'Yes, it was . . . No, not quite; it was lifting.'

Her chest felt tight. She felt she could choke. If her mother said just once more, 'And you were just sittin'?' she wouldn't be able to stand it. She would scream, louder than she had done downstairs when her father had brought the chain round her shoulders. Her mother repeating nearly everything she said was causing a muzzy dizziness in her head and she felt sick. She supposed it was the shock from the blow. She wanted to be alone, she wanted to be quiet and think. She knew she would have to think, for nothing would be the same again. The pretence was ended, at least for her. She didn't know if she could go on living in this house, even if he would let her. She didn't know whether the truth that had burst into her mind this morning would allow her to go on living here and look at them playing out their lives. She didn't think she could do it.

Her father's voice coming from the landing startled her. She knew he was in the bathroom and shouting at Willie in his bedroom. 'Dancin', clubs, jivin' . . . squares, beats and all the bloody rest of it and nobody in the house when they come home, nobody. There's things to be said on both sides. Is there any home life here? I ask you, is there? My wage is good enough to run this house, I've always said it. They come home from school and not a bloody soul in sight. They come home from the office and not a bloody soul in sight. An' the years roll on, an' where's the home life? Where is it, for anybody, I ask you? I've had it.'

Brid put her hands over her ears as her mother rushed to the door and tore it open, but she could not shut out her voice. 'Aye, and you'll have it again. You know the cure, don't you? Well, take it, but you're not stopping me goin' out. No, me lad. This is just an excuse to start again, isn't it? Well, you can save your breath. Stay in the house and wash and cook and sit and wait for you comin' in? That's what you want, isn't it? Sit in the house and sew a bloody fine seam at night while you're out at the club or some such. Oh no. You say you don't go out much. Not now, because you've got the tele—'

'Shall I open the windows?' It was Willie's voice low and sarcastic.

'Well, if you think I'm gonna take this lying down—' she was still yelling.

'You take more than that lying down.'

Their voices came, together now, Willie's and her mother's, Willie crying, 'Cut it out. Cut it out. What are you coming to, anyway?' and her mother screaming, 'You dirty swine! That's all you are, a dirty swine.'

As the bathroom door banged, her bedroom door opened again and Brid knew that her mother was standing with her back to it. Then she was standing over her whispering fiercely into her face, 'Look; whoever this man is, make sure he won't lead you hell. Do you hear? See what I've got? Make sure, I'm tellin' you, afore you take the step.'

Brid stared up into her mother's wild eyes. How silly she was, really. How silly. Why hadn't she made sure? Could anybody ever be sure? Oh, if she would only go away and leave her alone. The buzzing was loud in her head. It felt as if it would burst. She would never marry anybody. Never. Never. She would never let a man touch her . . .

'Even if you get yourself landed with something, don't take him as a loophole, but make sure.'

'Leave me alone. Please leave me alone; my neck's paining me and I want to go to sleep. Leave me alone.' If her mother didn't leave her alone she would scream at her. She would scream and shout like the rest of them. She had to restrain herself from pushing her mother's face away. She didn't like the look of it. The cheery, laughing expression was hard. The eyes and the mouth were just straight lines on a brittle surface. She shut her eyes.

Alice Stevens withdrew slowly from the bed and stood for a moment talking, as if to herself now, and about domestic things. 'I'll never be able to start the washing the day, and there's a pile there. But I just can't. And there's the dinner to see to an' all. Well, he can bloody well go hungry. That'll settle him. But all that washing.' . . .

The door closed and Brid lay still, looking into the pattern of colour upon her closed lids. Sunday. Sunday. Day of rest. She had always thought that there should be two Sundays in a week, one on which you didn't have to do the washing. The Pattersons across the road, the Crosbys and the Wrights, they never washed on a Sunday. Her Aunt Olive never washed on a Sunday. On the rare occasions when her mother referred to her Aunt Olive she would say she was damned lucky to be able to stay at home and do her washing during the week, that she was damned lucky in all ways in having a man like Uncle John who'd come home at night and do the washing up, as well as the ironing.

In spite of her effort to restrain it, her mind took her down the street and into the Palmers' house.

Her Aunt Olive was often off-colour. She had an ailment that had no name but which took her to bed for days at a time and gave her headaches and pains all over. When the ailment was bad her Uncle John would come home from work and help in the house; he was very good to her was her Uncle John. Over the last few years he had bought her a television, a fridge and a washing machine, and only recently he had added to the latter a spin dryer. The house was well furnished and bright, and Aunt Olive was always at home when her man came in. She was a home woman who doted on her family. She was proud of Harry and worried over Sandy, and she loved Uncle John and kept him tied to her by sympathy. But the house always seemed a happy one. Once, her dad, in a storm of abuse when fighting with her mother, had given a reason for this. He had said, 'Who wouldn't be happy with two women, one at home and one away, and not so far away at that?'

Perhaps it wouldn't have been so bad during the last few years, Brid thought, if her mother hadn't left her old job with the light industry and gone and got set on in the paper mills where Uncle John worked. Yet even after that, her Uncle John continued to drop into the house and her father continued to go out to the club with him. It wasn't understandable, it wasn't. One thing seemed to shout liar at the other. How could her father, knowing that her mother was going with his pal, talk to him, go out with him, remain in his company, evening after evening. The whole set-up made her feel sick in her stomach. Yet it was behind this supposedly tolerant façade that she had taken refuge for years. If there was anything going on her father simply wouldn't put up with it. Her father and her Uncle John would have rowed. But as far back as she could remember she knew it had been going on, and her father and Uncle John hadn't rowed, which made it more horrible still.

The pain in her neck was becoming worse. Her head was muddly. She again wanted to be sick. She turned on her side, and now, under the cover of the bedclothes, a face loomed up clear and close. It was Joe's face, and he said to her, 'You shouldn't stare like that, you should keep blinking and not look at the sun directly. Look away to the side. You were staring as if you were looking away beyond it, from where it comes.'

'From where it comes.' She said the words aloud, then burying her face in the pillow she gave way to a storm of weeping, muttering at intervals, 'I wish I was there . . . from where it comes. I wish I was dead. Oh, I do.'

Three

LONG AFTER BRID HAD DISAPPEARED DOWN THE road Joe continued to sit on the top of Stockwell Hill. He had never known such a dawn: everything was afloat in light; even the sea seemed wrenched from its bed and to be straining skywards. There was a lightness and floating quality about the whole earth, and as usual he began a commentary to himself with, 'By! it has been a bonny dawn.' But when his words were checked by reason of the added lustre to the morning, his commentary went on, 'Well, she *is* nice. I knew she was; I wasn't wrong.' From the moment he knew he was attracted to her, he began to take her to pieces. Look at the heels she wore; and she had admitted she would like to wear coloured stockings.

Fancy anyone wanting to put on red woollen stockings as if they were back in the fourteenth century. Funny, when you came to think about it, with the lot of them thinking they were the last second's delivery in time, so bloomin' up-to-date they couldn't be beaten, and then wearing coloured wool stockings. And her skirt showed her knees, like all the rest of them; you would swear they were wearing sawn-off crinolines. And she plucked her eyebrows. He wasn't against make-up, but when they plucked their eyebrows it was going too far. Yet on the Monday he had gone to George's coffee shop to see if she was there, and after talking to her he dissected no more; he knew she was all right.

It was hunger now that drove him homewards. He didn't go by the road but ran down the hill towards the beach, slithering and stumbling when the hill became very steep in its descent towards the sand. The sand was soft and dry and made walking slow, and the rim of the water seemed much further away than it had done from his perch up above. He crossed over from the dry sand to the wet and watched his feet now imprinting swift dark patterns.

From the top of the hill the distance towards the warning notice had looked nothing, but it took him nearly ten minutes to reach it. He glanced at the notice as he passed. The pole to which it was attached was leaning sideways; the faded letters on the board were still readable: 'DANGER. DO NOT BATHE BEYOND THIS

POINT.' He smiled at it. His father had introduced him to bathing here and the notice had been lop-sided then. When he reached the bay, hemmed in by the half-circle of rocks, he stopped for a moment to gaze at it. On a morning such as this, if his father had been alive, they would both have been in there rolling and sporting like two lads, not like father and son at all. The sand leading into the water of the bay dipped swiftly away from his feet at this point. That was why even when the tide was out you could always have enough water to mess about in. The tide left no impression on the bay, for it was as if at one time a giant hand had scooped out a hollow in the sand where the water would remain against falling tides.

As he stood looking over the bay he sniffed, then turned his head to look back up the beach which here sloped upwards to a deep copse of trees, black now against the bright light. He had smelt the wonderful aroma of bacon frying. Someone was likely camping out in the woods up there. Glory! Couldn't he eat some of that.

He turned about and quickly made towards the trees. The scramble up to them was nothing compared with the scramble down Stockwell Hill, for it was merely a gentle rise from the beach. When he entered the comparative darkness of the trees he stood blinking and sniffing for a moment. Whoever was there, he couldn't expect them to dish out any of their bacon, but they might likely be good for a cup of tea. If they offered him one he wouldn't say no. By lad! he wouldn't. He hadn't realised how hungry and thirsty he was.

He followed the direction of the appetising smell, and it led him to the middle of the copse, then onward to its edge; and there, disappointed at not having espied a tent and campers, he stopped and looked towards the dark shape of the car parked on the verge of the trees. As he approached it he could see a woman sitting on a low camping chair with a plate on her lap, and a man sitting on the car step balancing a plate on his knee. A spirit stove, on which stood a tin kettle, was nearby, and the place around them was littered with objects that gave the appearance of a house without walls.

'Good-morning.'

They both looked up at him and answered, 'Good-morning;' and the man added, 'And it's a grand one too, isn't it?'

His voice was high. He was evidently not from these parts. Joe passed on, thinking, if they had offered him a cup of tea he wouldn't have taken it. They looked slovenly, dirty, somehow.

He arrived home to find his mother up and the breakfast set, and as he threw his cap on to the sofa and looked towards the table he exclaimed, 'By lad! I'm ready for this.'

Annie Lloyd turned from the stove to look at her son and asked, 'Well! where have you been this time?'

It was as if he had just been out for an hour's stroll. With practice she was able to hide the fears that these midnight jaunts of her son created in her. It had been all right when he had gone along with his father, but even then she hadn't cared much for them jaunting off in the middle of the night; yet she had made no adverse comment on the escapades; men were men and had oddities in them. If you were wise you respected the oddities, and it was made easier when you loved your man. But her husband and son jaunting off for walks in the middle of the night was a different thing altogether to the lad going alone. He had been at it for three years now, but she still could not get used to it and always experienced a sense of relief when he was home again. His going down the pit did not fill her with the same apprehension as did his midnight rambling; there were others down the pit, whereas on these ramblings he was alone.

After Joe had washed his hands and face he returned to the kitchen and sat down with a flop on the couch. Putting his hands behind his head he lay back and let out a long breath as he said, 'It's a grand morning.'

'Yes, it is a grand morning. It's going to be hot. It's hot already.'

'There's a breeze coming up; it'll turn to a wind this afternoon, you'll see. It'll still be hot, though.'

'Come on, sit up.'

He pulled himself up with a jerk and took his seat

71

at the table, but before he attacked the two eggs and three rashers of bacon reposing on the dinner plate he glanced quickly over the table as if for the first time he was noticing its shining quality. Everything seemed to be brighter this morning, or was it just him? No. The table was shining, and he realised that his home was a shining place. Always clean and spotless. His mother was clean and spotless too. As he chewed on a mouthful of rich-flavoured bacon, causing his digestive juices to fill his mouth so full he had to keep his lips closed while he ate, he looked towards his mother where she was standing pouring out the tea, and it came to him with a jerk of surprise that she was young, still young. She was thirty-seven, but she was still young. She had a nice figure. Perhaps her hips were a bit too big, but that was with sitting doing the dressmaking. She was a wizard with her needle and had done dressmaking for people for years. It had stood her in good stead after his dad had died. She was wearing a pink patterned dress, and again he thought, from her back view she could have been taken for a young girl. Even full-faced she could have passed for a young woman, until you looked into her eyes. They were blue and clear, but they had an expression in them that denied youth. Joe had noticed this before, but never questioned it further than to think his mother's eyes were strained with the sewing and that she should give it up. But now he paused in his eating as she handed him a cup of tea. Although she was smiling at him, the look was still there and he could name it now: his mother was lonely. He hadn't thought about her being lonely, for she was always so busy. Fancy, it had never struck him before. He seemed to be noticing lots of things this morning. It was as if he had lost a skin and was more sensitive than ever to the atmosphere about him. His mother was lonely. Had she always been lonely? He could always remember that look in her eyes. But his dad had loved her, loved her dearly, passionately should be the word, but he didn't like to say that in connection with his parents. Yet she had always had that look about the eyes. Was it because his dad went roaming at night when his shift allowed? Maybe. He had never thought about it. Funny, he had just never thought about it. Had his dad thought about it, that his wife was lonely? He couldn't have or he wouldn't have left her. Not his dad. That was why she wanted to marry Mr Bishop, because she was lonely. To his own surprise he heard himself talking quickly, rapidly, leaning across the table to her as he did so. 'I've been thinking' – although he hadn't, but was merely releasing an emotional pressure – 'You go ahead and do what you want. Don't mind me. I'll be all right. Things'll work out. You just go ahead and make your own arrangements and I'll fit in.'

She had stopped eating and was staring at him, and he watched the blue of her eyes become paler behind

a mist, and her voice had a break in it as she said, 'But
. . . but you know it'll mean leaving this house?'

'Well, what about it? You've always hankered after
a modern one. Now, you have.' He nodded at her
and laughed, trying to bring the subject on to a
lighter footing. 'Anyway—' he bent his head over
the plate and, taking up a forkful of food, chewed
on it vigorously for a few moments before adding,
'who knows, I might stay here meself.'

'What d'you mean? Joe, look at me. What d'you
mean?'

He looked at her, his eyes twinkling. 'I've got a
girl.'

'You've got a girl?' Her voice was soft.

'Yes.' He put his knife and fork down and pushed
his plate to one side, and hitching his chair towards
the corner of the table so that his outstretched hand
could touch hers, he said, 'She's nice, Mam. You know
something? She's nothing like you yet, but she's goin'
to be, she's goin' to be. I know she is.'

She smiled softly at him, the while shaking her head.
'Is that a recommendation?'

'Aw, go on; you're only fishin'.'

'How old is she?'

'Seventeen.'

'But you're only nineteen . . . Are you serious,
Joe?'

'Me dad married you when he was eighteen,

remember? And I'll be twenty in six weeks' time. And yes, I'm serious, Mam. You know me. I've kept away from them 'cos I didn't seem to be able to find the right one.'

'But don't you think you should go out with a number before . . .?'

'No. No, I don't. I don't believe in that theory at all. That's the theory of the high-fliers. I hear it down below every day. "Test and try, man," they say. "Test and try afore you buy." No, Mam; that's not for me. And I knew as soon as I saw her; at least, not long after.'

'What's her name?'

'Brid Stevens.'

'Brid?'

'Short for Bridget. She said her mother had to call her Bridget after her mother-in-law, Brid's grannie: her grannie was buying the pram, and unless the child was called after her, no pram. She can be funny, she can't tell a tale without laughing . . . she can be funny.'

'Are you going to bring her along home?'

'I'd like to, Mam.'

'What about this afternoon?'

'Fine, I'm meeting her along at the bay. We're going to have a swim. We should be back here about fourish. All right?'

'All right with me.'

They smiled at each other, and now Joe pulled his

plate back towards him and continued to eat the congealing remains of his breakfast.

As his mother stood up to pour out more tea she asked him, 'Did you walk far?'

'Quite a way.'

'You tired?'

'No; I'm as fresh as a daisy.'

'I was thinking about going to church this morning, would you like to come?'

'Oh lordy! Mam, I *am* tired.'

As he lay back in his chair laughing, her hand came out and gently boxed his ear, and they both laughed. Then he said quietly, 'No, Mam; count me out. I'll come some time. As I said afore, I'll go one of these mornings on the spur of the moment and I won't know why. But, thanks all the same, not this morning. Fact is, I *am* tired . . . it's true. Yes, honest. I'm done in. I'm going to bed and I'll sleep until dinner time. Will you wake me around twelve? I want to be out by half-past one. All right?'

'All right.' As she passed him she touched his head softly and he put his hand up swiftly and caught her fingers and tightly squeezed them for a moment. It was a gesture that his father had been wont to make, and after it the kitchen was filled with a sweet, full silence. He went and sat on the couch and put his head back and yawned and stretched his arms. He was filled with joy, a new kind of joy: it was like a promise, a golden promise. A ray of sun shining through the kitchen window fell across his face and he took it as a seal on that promise. Life was to be full of light and wonder. This was living. This was loving, he thought as he climbed the stairs to his bedroom.

His mother called him at twelve o'clock and he woke immediately to her touch.

'Ossie's been,' she said.

'Yes? . . . Oh, lord.'

'He said for you not to miss the quarter to two bus. I didn't say anything.'

'I'd forgotten; but I didn't promise him anything. I just said if I felt like it . . . And I don't feel like it. Not today.' He smiled shyly at his mother. 'You mentioned nothing?'

'No, not a word.' She pressed her lips together as she gave him a confederate's smile.

'By, I'm glad of that. He would have chaffed the lugs off me all week. He'll have to know some time, I suppose; though that can wait. But I didn't want him to know so soon, for things aren't settled yet. With me they are, but not with her . . . I haven't sort of spoken. You know what I mean?'

'Yes, I know what you mean.' She patted his shoulder and left the room, and immediately he got out of bed. There was no bathroom in the house, and after donning a pair of old trousers he went downstairs to wash in the scullery. When he returned to his room he selected his best suit, even though he knew he'd have it off before he saw her and that it would be lying on the rocks getting creased. But still, he would be fetching her home and the occasion demanded his best suit.

At dinner his mother said jokingly, 'If you're going in the water you'd better not eat so much,' and he replied on a laugh, 'Why? I've never sunk yet. And never left a dirty plate, either.'

Suddenly, as if her mind had never left the subject, she said, 'Is she serious? I mean . . . well, you know what I mean, don't you?'

'Well, she dances the modern stuff, jive and all that, and makes up, and wears them stiletto heels, but she's all right. I know she's all right, Mam. Something tells me.'

'Where did you meet her?'

'At the club in South Scardyke.'

'The club?' There was a slight raising of his mother's eyebrows and he put in quickly, 'Yes, I know what you're thinking; about the lot that goes there. She was among them but on the side, if you know what I mean?'

'Does she drink?'

'Yes, coffee, and she likes it strong . . . Aw Mam, don't worry, you'll see her for yourself in an hour or two.' He was detecting a change in his mother's attitude, as if she had done a lot of thinking during the time he had been in bed and now, and was a little worried. But he wasn't displeased with her attitude. It showed she wasn't so taken up with her own affairs that she could let his slide. He said now, 'Mind if I go?'

'No; get yourself away. And I'll have the tea on the table at half-past four, mind.'

'Half-past four it'll be, on the doorstep. You have the word of a Lloyd, Madam.' He saluted her, and she laughed and pushed him away.

He took up his jacket from the back of the chair and put it on and adjusted his tie, then asked, preening himself, 'How do I look?'

'No different from usual that I can see.' She shook her head with mock primness, then added seriously, 'But why you want to put your good suit on to go down to the beach puzzles me.'

'Does it? Then, Mrs Lloyd, you're dim. Goodbye, Mrs Lloyd.'

'Oh, away with you!'

He bent swiftly to her and gave her a rare kiss, and she remained still, making no more remarks. And he went out, closing the door quietly behind him.

He strolled down the village street. It was quiet with a Sunday quiet that hits most places around noon: everyone was indoors eating. The houses in the centre of the village, the original part of Johnson's Cross, looked mellow. They were all built of rough quarry stone, the colour of which time had blended to a deep thick cream. He liked the village; he wished he would never have to leave it. But then if . . . The 'if' presented the future to him, and he said to himself, 'Well, I'll just have to, won't I?' And the answer caused an excitement in his stomach and quickened his step, and as he took the short cuts across the fields to the beach, he almost skipped.

When he came to the outskirts of the copse to where he had seen the motorists breakfasting that morning, he stopped and looked at the ground, then exclaimed aloud, 'By lad! you would think they would have the sense and decency to clear up after them. I bet that pair's left their trademark across the country.' He went on and was just about to enter the copse when the glint of something bright lying in the long grass to the left of him brought him to a stop. The glint was from the handlebar of a motor-bike. He took a couple of steps out of his way and ascertained that, yes, there was not just one motor-bike, there were three, and he muttered, 'Bust it!' for the motor-bikes meant there were fellows already down in the bay. Well, whoever they were, they mightn't stay long; perhaps they were just passing through and had gone down for a dip. Very likely they knew of this place. Of course they would have to know of it, for no one passing this bit of woodland would think that just beyond lay the sea. People never thought of the sea until they saw it from the open ground. Well, he supposed, if the worst came to the worst the bay would be big enough for four people . . . five. Five, he reminded himself.

Where the copse became more of a thicket, he saw the bundles of clothing. They were in three separate piles, yet similar, two pairs of black sail-cloth trousers being identical. The sight of them brought a strange uneasiness to him.

The sound of yelling voices brought him clear of the thicket to the top of the bank leading down to the beach, and there, picking their way tentatively on bare feet over the rocks towards him, were two of the Palmer gang, as he thought of Ronnie Fitzsimmons and Clarky Leach, with Sandy Palmer himself trailing behind. So taken up were they by the rough ascent that they did not become aware of Joe until they were within a few yards of him; and then it was Clarky Leach who, lifting his head, saw him first. He had been negotiating the rough gulley on all fours when, pretending to be a dog, he lifted his head backwards and sniffed; and it was then he saw Joe; and he stopped in his crawling to exclaim on a high, reedy note, 'Coo! fellas. Look who's here!'

Ronnie Fitzsimmons was the next to see Joe and he said, 'It's Joe.' The reference could have indicated that he was welcoming a pal, but he then added, 'Lloyd' and it took away the seeming friendliness from his use of the Christian name.

Sandy Palmer was standing on one foot extracting a piece of dry seaweed from between his toes when he heard the name, and his head shot up so quickly that he almost overbalanced. He stood staring up the rocky incline towards the slight, neatly dressed figure of Joe Lloyd . . . Joe Lloyd. All morning he had been thinking of Joe Lloyd. It was as if his thinking had conjured him up out of the air. His feelings remained stationary and numbed for a moment with surprise. Dinner time on a Sunday at the bay, and there he was all dressed up as if he were going into town. It seemed odd, very odd. It came into his mind that he might have been praying all the morning and his prayers had been answered. The surprise faded away, and the fury that had been raging in him, the fury that had driven him out of the house without his Sunday dinner returned, its force making him tremble. All morning he had wanted to smash into something, to hit out at something, to hurt something, to ease the gnawing ache inside him. He did not recognise it as an ache but as a desire to rend and tear. He had been in this state for three weeks, although the feeling had been nothing compared with what he had experienced today. He began to climb upwards towards the copse now, his body straight. His feet ignoring the sharpness of the rocks, he walked as straight as if he were lording it through the town with his hands in his narrow pockets.

When he stood before Joe his pals were already

one on each side of him, and he stared at Joe through narrowed slits before he said, 'What are you after here?'

'After? Nothing.' There was a trace of nervousness in Joe's voice, and he looked to each side of him, then back to Sandy Palmer before adding, 'Nothing . . . well, that is, the same as you, I'm goin' to bathe.'

'Bathe? What, in them!' Ronnie Fitzsimmons flicked his forefinger up the sleeve of Joe's jacket.

'Where's your towel and things?' It was like an interrogation, and Joe, looking straight into Sandy Palmer's tight face, said, 'I've never used a towel, I let the water dry on me.'

'He lets the water dry on him.' Sandy Palmer was not looking at Joe now but at his pals, first at Ronnie Fitzsimmons, and then his eyes, leaping over the top of Joe's head, came to Clarky Leach, and he repeated, 'He lets the water dry on him.'

Joe began to tremble. It was just a small reaction at first in his thighs, not noticeable in his face and hands, but it told him he was afraid. One of them he could have managed. With two of them he would have stood a poor chance. With three of them and Sandy Palmer in the lead he knew his position was hopeless. So he tried diplomacy. Forcing a smile to his face and an airy tone to his voice, he asked, 'Is it cold?'

No-one answered him. The two satellites looked towards their leader, and when he did not speak they took their cue from him, and Ronnie Fitzsimmons repeated, with the irritating stupidity of the dull-witted, 'He says, is it cold? Sandy.'

Sandy's eyes were wide open now. They were brown, almost black-hued, and should have been bright and sparkling, if only because he had just come out of the sea, but there was no sparkle in them. They looked dull, opaque, as if light had never passed through them. They were eyes coloured with frustration. Whatever change took place in them was brought about by strong emotion only. The eyes darkened still further now as he said, 'You're a swab.'

Joe made no reply but the trembling in his thighs moved downwards towards his knees.

'D'you hear what Sandy says? You're a swab.' Ronnie Fitzsimmons accompanied this statement with a thrust of his elbow that, for a moment, knocked Joe off-balance and took him a couple of steps away from them. Immediately they brought the distance between them back to what it was before.

'What were you doing last night . . . all night?'

'Last night?' Joe blinked up at the tall naked figure before him, and paused as if he was thinking, then said, 'I was walking.'

'He was walking.' Clarky Leach bounced his head towards his two pals and repeated, 'D'you hear that, Sandy? he was walkin' . . . he was walkin' all night.'

'Shut up!' Sandy Palmer continued to stare at Joe.

Walking; he said he had been walking. Does a fella walk when he's got Brid Stevens with him? The ache that had been in him for weeks now sharpened itself until he felt it like an actual stab under his ribs. The very thought of Brid caused an active boiling inside him, and he wanted to hit out with both his hands and his feet: he wanted to tear into shreds the smooth face confronting him. Brid had been with this fella all night . . . Ever since he had been at school he had wanted Brid Stevens. He had even played a game with himself, saying, 'Aw, let her wait. There's plenty of time, an' plenty of others.' And he had gone round with others. Susie Wright . . . he had gone round with her for six months solid, while all the time being conscious of Brid down the street. Then there came the actual moment when he realised he couldn't play games with himself any more. It was time to make a move, for Brid had something that was attracting others. She hadn't taken to his advances at all, but this only put an edge to his appetite. That time when, coming back from the club – yes he had even left the club early to see her back so that her old man wouldn't go on – he had made up to her and she had turned on him, hit out at him she had, and he had laughed at her. He hadn't minded that; it proved she wasn't easy. He was glad to find that she wasn't loose-legged.

That night, their Harry had passed them in the street, and after Brid had plunged into the house and he was going back to the club to get a dance in before twelve, their Harry had called from the garden, 'Here a minute!' and he had gone back.

'Walk down the road,' said Harry. And he had walked down the road in the opposite direction from the club.

'You mad!' said Harry.

'What d'you mean, me mad?'

'Brid Stevens.'

'What about Brid?'

'Are you plain bats?'

'What're you gettin' at?'

They had stopped at the far corner of the street under a lamp-post, and Harry had peered at him, then whispered, 'You don't know?'

'Know what? What the hell is it I should know?'

'Good God!'

'What the hell you good-Godding for? What's up with you? What should I know?'

'Well, I thought you knew about the old man.'

'Which old man? Brid's old man or our old man?'

'Our old man.'

'Well, for Christ's sake! what's wrong with him? Spit it out.'

'Don't be such a dim bugger. He fathered Brid; she's our half-sister. That's what all this business has been about for years: me mother bein' bad all the time and old Stevens driving everybody daft . . . Don't look like that; I thought you knew. And when I saw you with her, well, I –'

'Shut up! Shut your flaming mouth!'

He had turned and run until he was puffed. Then he had walked for a long time, all the while thinking, not of Brid, but of his father, and the desire to kill him was stronger than any feeling he'd had in his life before.

After that, he hadn't kept out of Brid's way but had tormented her every time he saw her, until he realised that, half-sister or no half-sister, it made no difference to his feelings, and he would have to do something about it . . . Something. But what? He had been groping in his mind about the something when he came downstairs this morning and his mother, brighter than usual, had imparted the news to him: 'There was hell let loose in the Stevenses',' she said. 'That Brid has been out all night with a fella.' He had wanted to hit his mother. He had known without being told the name of the fella. It was Joe Lloyd. He had come to the club two Saturdays running and had been in George's a number of times during the last couple of weeks, and each time she had sat nattering to him. And now, right here, dead plonk in front of him, was Joe Lloyd, and he had been out all night with Brid.

Like a flash of lightning, his hands went out and grabbed a fistful of Joe's jacket lapel, tie and shirt. The impact was so sudden that Joe would have fallen over backwards had not the grip on his clothes steadied him, and he put his hands up to his collar and strained his neck as he cried, 'Give over! you're choking me. Give over!'

'You had Brid Stevens with you, hadn't you? Come on, hadn't you?'

'No ... No, only this –' A vicious shake, which jerked his head backwards, cut off the remainder of his words and he choked, then coughed and gasped. When he was again steady he was breathing as hard as if he had run a fast mile across the fells, and he just heard the tail-end of Clarky Leach's remark coming from way back, high in his nose: 'With Brid Stevens?' And he knew that whatever knowledge Sandy Palmer possessed was not shared by his two mates, because Ronnie Fitzsimmons was now verifying it: 'Coo! You little stinker, you. Fancy that. Him and Brid out all night. Coo! you dirty little bastard.'

'I wasn't.' Joe gasped. 'We weren't. Not all night. We –'

'Just long enough to have some fun, eh?' He was being shaken again; but this time he did not suffer it. For a moment his fear fled and righteous anger took its place. With a sudden tug he freed himself from Sandy Palmer's grasp.

He had got his release through the element of surprise, and it was shown on the boys' faces as he confronted them. He was a couple of yards away from them now but bending towards them in a crouching movement, and his voice was no longer conciliatory.

'You lay your hands on me again and you'll see what you'll get. That goes for all of you. Now mind, I'm tellin' you. Don't think you can come your gang warfare on me. It's like you to go around in threes; you're frightened to tackle anyone single. I'll take you on any day of the week, Palmer, alone, if you've got that much spunk.'

'Listen to him! Listen to him!' In a sideward glance, Clarky's eyes came to rest on Sandy Palmer, who was standing as still as if he had been frozen to the spot.

Clarky was waiting for a cue from his leader, and in the next second he got it.

'Get him!'

Like three wolves, the boys pounced on Joe, who was instantly borne to the ground, and quickly his struggles were checked by Sandy Palmer sitting on his legs and by the other two holding his arms spreadeagled on the ground. They were all panting, and Clarky gasped, 'What you going to do with him, Sandy?'

Sandy was staring down into the now blazing face of Joe and he said quietly, 'You'll see. Take his clothes off.'

Joe made an attempt to struggle again, but finding this useless, he used the only weapon left to him, his voice. With a bellow that even shook his attackers, he yelled, 'Help! Help!' and as his lips framed the word

'Police!' Ronnie Fitzsimmon's hand clapped across them. 'Where's something to stuff in his mouth?'

Sandy Palmer motioned to Clarky Leach, saying, 'Go and get our things.'

Within a minute the clothes were being dumped down to the side of Joe, and Sandy Palmer said, 'Pass me me hanky here.'

Joe bit ineffectively at the hand that rammed the handkerchief into his mouth. Then his trousers and his short underpants were torn off, and Ronnie Fitzsimmons exclaimed, 'Look! he's got his trunks on. He was going in all right.'

Suddenly, Joe became still; the fight went out of him, and the trembling now reached every pore of his body.

'He'll go in all right.'

The words brought to Joe the quality of danger attached to this part of the coast. He had never before sensed it so clearly. What would they do? Dump him over the rocks into the gut?

Suddenly, he began to pray, the prayers he had learned at Sunday school. God of mercy, God who gave to the world his only begotten Son, Have mercy on me . . . Jesus, Jesus, Jesus.

'Look out and see if there's anybody down below.' Sandy Palmer jerked his head in the direction of the beach, and Clarky Leach ran to the end of the copse, then came back again panting. 'You can't take him

down there, Sandy. There's a man and woman lyin'
just along on the sands, not far. They're picnickin' an'
the fella's been in; he's sunbathing.'

Sandy Palmer stared into Joe's sweating face for a
moment, then looked about him as if searching for an
idea. And seemingly he found it. 'You got any string,
Clarky?' he said.

'String, Sandy? No.'

'You, Ronnie?'

'Might be a bit in me bag on me saddle.'

'Skip an' see.'

'What? Like this? I'd better put me clothes on; the
bike's near the road.'

'Put 'em on, then! Here, give him to me.' Sandy
Palmer took over his pal's position and his grip was
fiercer on Joe, so much so that Joe's face screwed up
with the agony of his cramped muscles.

When Fitzsimmons was dressed in his scanty attire
of tight trousers, tight singlet and anorak, he scuttled
through the trees to his motor-bike, and within a few
minutes returned with three pieces of cord of different
lengths.

'These do, Sandy?'

After glancing at the cord, Sandy said, 'Hang on
here again until I get me things on,' and again they
changed over. But all the while he was dressing he
kept his eyes on Joe. Next he gave the order to
Clarky Leach to get into his things, and again, when

his grip took over from Leach's, Joe's body writhed in agony.

There was an unrestrained terror in Joe now; he was whimpering inside, gabbling to himself in his fear: God! God! What would they do? Oh, Mam! If only somebody would come. He's a fiend, a fiend. Hellish! But what's he up to? He can't take me down to the bay.

His thoughts were jostled as he was dragged to his feet, and when he realised that they were going to tie him to a tree his eyes almost popped out of his head; and he made one final effort. Supported by his fear, he curved his back and heaved his stomach upwards in an effort to wrench himself free from them; but he succeeded only in straining himself. When they pulled him straight again he found he wasn't against the big tree but between two slender young ones. He struggled madly as the other two held him while Sandy Palmer tied one of his wrists and an ankle to one of the trunks; but his struggling ceased when Sandy Palmer, with an upward lift, wrenched his other leg toward the second tree, for the scream that tore through his body even penetrated the gag in his mouth, and for a moment he felt nothing and saw nothing.

'Coo! look, careful Sandy; he's passed out.'

A thrust from Sandy Palmer's fist under Joe's chin showed that he had not quite passed out, and when the long, thin fingers clamped his cheeks inwards, Joe opened his eyes and looked dazedly at his tormentor.

'What if somebody comes?' There was just a trace of apprehension in Clarky Leach's voice now.

Sandy Palmer took no notice of this question. He seemed deaf to the fear in his pal's voice and blind to everything but the youth in front of him. And now words squeezed themselves up through his neck and between his teeth: 'I'll larn you to take a young kid out all night. I'll larn you. You won't do it again, will you?' The hand shook viciously, and Joe's head with it. 'An' what were you doin' crawling along here with these on, eh?' He pulled out the elastic on Joe's bathing trunks with his forefinger and let it snap back viciously into Joe's stomach. 'Goin' to meet her, eh? An' goin' for a bathe together, eh? To wash out last night's business, eh?' The elastic band was pulled forward again, this time with such force that the woollen material of the leg was split, although the band remained. Then with a flick of his wrist Sandy Palmer drew out a knife from his back pocket and the blade seemed to present itself of its own volition. And when it was thrust under the band to split the elastic, the point seered the skin just as it was meant to. Each pore in Joe's body screamed in response and the groan again came through the handkerchief.

'Eeh! Sandy, man, lay off; you'll split his guts. Look, he's bleedin'.'

Again the leader made no response, but he calmly took a cigarette packet from his hip pocket and, standing close to Joe, he extracted a cigarette and lit it. It was at this point that a screaming began in Joe's mind. He knew what this meant. The word Jesus, Jesus, Jesus, raced around inside his head, intermingled with, Help me! Save me! Oh God. God save me. Bring somebody. Oh, Mam!

He closed his eyes tightly as he waited, and when the warm smoke wafted over his face he did not think of Sandy Palmer and his intentions, but strangely he was reminded of the last time he was in church. It wasn't his own church, but a high church in Hexham. His mother was with him; they were on a trip; and it was only her presence that had kept him in his seat, for as he listened to the preacher prattling on about Christ crucified, he was saying to himself, What good is this going to do me? I'd get much more good out of a tramp across the fells. And when the censer was being swung he had felt faint and wanted air. Outside, his mother had remarked, 'It was a very good sermon,' and he had answered, 'How I'm making it out now is that there's been more than one man crucified. They seemed to do it every day during the last war. I've been reading about Belsen,' which had shocked his mother, and she had come back at him straightway with, 'It isn't the same. He was different.'

The smoke was hot now on his face, and behind

the racing, screaming matter that was now his brain lay a quiet section, and it was still occupied with that Sunday he had been to church. His mother had said, 'He felt like a man, but He was God.' Now the screaming penetrated the quiet section and it hollered, 'Anybody who goes through this comes out qualified to be a god.' It might seem impossible to make sense out of anything he was thinking, and yet he understood: nobody going through this would be the same again, not to themselves or to anyone else; nobody afterwards would think the same of them because they would only have to look into their eyes to know they had qualified to be a . . . 'Go–d!'

The scream, denied full utterance through his mouth, poured itself out through his skin; when the cigarette touched his flesh his nerves screamed themselves into sweat.

'Eeh! Sandy. God! man. You'll maim him . . . Give over . . . Look; I'm off.'

'You stay where you are.'

The copse became quiet. The two boys stood away from the stretched figure and their leader. Their eyes were fixed on the quivering, seared flesh between the naked loins. They gazed in petrified fascination, yet their bodies were half turned as if for flight; and then Clarky's quick ear caught a sound. It was a scraping of a foot on the rocks and he jerked round and ran to the edge of the clearing. There he saw a bent figure scrambling up the bank and his mouth dropped into a wide gape. The next second he was with his pals again.

'Sandy, it's her! It's Brid! She's here.' Clarky flung his arm backwards as if to indicate Brid.

Sandy Palmer did not even glance towards Clarky, but, his eyes darting once more over Joe, he called quickly, 'Out of it!'

The other two needed no second warning; they were off and would have made for their motor-bikes but that Sandy's arm waved them down behind a clump of bushes, and there they waited.

And Joe waited. His whole body was crying with pain. His mind was screaming with a mixture of anger and fear and the tears were running down his face. As he waited he looked away sideways in the direction of the sea. In the dawn of this morning he had felt a man. He had sat on a hill and looked at the dawn, and at his side had sat the girl who not only his body but also his spirit had told him was for him. He had wanted her to see him as somebody different, not as the little meek chap Joe Lloyd, not the open-air chap Joe Lloyd, not the chap who talked poetry but couldn't write it. He wanted her to see him as the man, Joe Lloyd. The man who she would feel was for her. A man of strength despite his size, a man of beauty despite his size, for his limbs were smooth and compact, and his skin was warm and sunburned from his feet upwards to the top of his thighs and upwards again from his navel. But how would she see him now, trussed like a drying rabbit skin, stark naked and with his privates still quivering from the burning cigarette end? His spirit bowed itself down low under the humiliation. It too was crying.

And there she was, coming out of the full sun into the dappled shade of the copse. He did not droop his head when her horror-filled gaze brought her to a dead, gaping stop. Then her head, pushing itself back on her shoulders, looked for a moment as if it would topple her backwards.

The look in her eyes brought a groan from Joe, for in her gaze was reflected the dirt of life, the dirt from which he had always washed his hands. Even in thought he had tried to keep away from the dirt of life. He had wanted to think of life as fine, grand, beautiful. This complex dream desire, this God-given yet God-forbidden instinct which came into evidence from the moment the lips suckled the breast, this spring of interest and curiosity that disturbed the adolescent mind, this promise of the body for ecstatic wonder . . . this was the one thing he had tried to keep clean. So much had aimed to soil it. The talk of the lads at school. The lavatories, and Ernie Bowen pressing against him. Bill Chaters and Frankie Potter talking on the backshifts. And the TV: the girls wearing only tights, bending backwards and wriggling their thighs to the camera. He had wondered for a while about these cameramen focussing the light on them, but dismissed it with the thought, They won't see it like that, it's just a job. But now he knew his efforts were as nothing, for he was seeing himself reflected in Brid's horrified gaze.

When she screamed he screwed his eyes up, and he kept them screwed even when he heard her gasping breath near him.

'Joe. Oh Joe. Oh my God! Joe. Oh, I can't get it loose. Oh God in heaven! Oh, the devils! The beasts! The beasts!'

Slowly Joe opened his eyes and looked at her. She was struggling ineffectively with the cords at his wrists, hurting him more as she tried to release him. She had not thought to take the gag out of his mouth, and as he made a motion with his head to draw her attention to his face, his own attention was caught by the sight of a man now entering the copse. He too was naked but for bathing trunks. For a minute he stood still with his hands extended away from his sides; then seemingly in a couple of leaps he was standing beside Brid, and he too was using the name of God, but going further, crying, 'God Almighty! God Almighty!' And to this he added, 'The bastards!'

It was hardly a word that a schoolteacher should use, but Leonard Morley was in the habit of using it frequently. Hardly a day passed but he would exclaim to himself, 'The young bastards!' It hadn't always been like this. He could look back to the time when he had liked young lads, when he had said that Robson, or Wheatley, or Colleridge was a lad, a young devil, but still a lad. The term 'lad' in itself had indicated that the boy in question was a bit of a devil. And the devil had indicated that the lad was an outsize of a lad. He could remember going home to Phyllis when they were first married and saying, 'What d'you think happened to-day? Some devil took Sefton's bike to pieces, completely to pieces. It looked as if it was in a thousand bits. I thought he would have taken off, the explosion was so great.' The funny side of this had been that Sefton was the gym instructor and advocated walking. And then there was the day that one of the lads with a knack for it had swapped some wiring around. He must have got into the school on the Sunday, and what happened on the Monday morning, especially in the chemmy lab, wasn't forgotten for a long, long time. The lads then had been devils . . . but they weren't bastards. He couldn't actually remember the time when they had changed to being bastards, although he knew it wasn't directly after the war, but in the early sixties, he would say.

He tore at the cords fastening the boy to the tree and as he worked he talked rapidly. 'Who did this? How long have you been here? If you can get them they'll do years for this. My God! I would like to see them on the receiving end of a birch.' He put his arms underneath Joe to support him and half carried him out beyond the copse to the grass. He seemed unaware of Brid, and yet, after he had laid Joe down he looked up at her and said with a note of command, 'Run to the bank and call my wife.'

From where she was standing, her eyes fixed on Joe's pale, averted face, Brid did not seem to hear his words, and the man, realising this, put his hand to his mouth and called, 'Phyllis! Phyllis!'

As the call died away there came a movement from away behind them in the direction of the road, but he could see nothing.

There now followed the sound of motor cycles starting up, and on hearing it Brid bit into her lower lip for she knew, as plainly as if she had seen them, who the riders were.

Joe did not hear the machines. He was conscious only of pain and his nakedness, and to remove this from Brid's eyes he turned with an effort on to his face. Although his legs were pressed tightly together and his arms were hugging his body, his limbs still had the feeling of being stretched, and added to this was the sensation of a hot wire being drawn through the marrow of his bones. He wanted to slip away into oblivion; it would have been easy, for he was faint and sick. His mouth, which also still retained that stretched feeling, moved about some words, and the man kneeling on the grass and bending his ears to him said, 'What is it?'

'Me clothes.'

'Where did you leave them?'

His jaws moved twice before he brought out, 'About . . . somewhere.'

The man looked back to where the torn trunks lay between the slender trees and he moved hastily forward and picked them up, then went behind the few bushes, looking here and there.

The fingers of Brid's left hand were pressing upwards across her mouth, and her thumb was dug in under her cheek bone. The fingers were aiming to press down the fear that was filling her and which was attempting to escape in a gabble of words, a gabble of names which, strangely enough, did not include Sandy Palmer's. It was her mother's name, her father's name, and the name of her Uncle John which raced about in her mind, and would escape if she did not prevent them.

Her eyes travelled down from the back of Joe's head to his buttocks. They were small and firm and pale compared with the skin of his back and that of his legs. The soles of his feet were turned upwards and in this moment she was surprised that she could register the fact that they were without corn or callus. They were broad-soled, flat yet shapely, the feet of a walker . . . But her mother, and her father, and her Uncle John. Her mother and her father and her Uncle

John: the words were spiralling higher in her head, but the man stopped them from escaping by making his appearance once again with Joe's clothes across his arm, just as a woman pulled herself up over the top of the bank as Brid herself had done only a few minutes earlier on her hands and knees. And when she straightened up, the man called to her: 'Here! Phyllis; come and look at this. No wonder she screamed. They had him gagged and spreadeagled between these trees.' He pointed. 'You wouldn't believe it . . . or would you? It's what I've been saying all along, they're not human any more.' He approached the woman, talking as if Brid and Joe weren't there, and then he turned with her and came towards them again.

'They were fellows on motor-bikes, I heard them go off. Couldn't have been anybody but them. Look at this.' He bent down and his hands came gently on to Joe's shoulder, and his voice changed now as he said softly, 'Turn over, boy, let my wife see. Don't worry, she's been a nurse.'

Joe, after turning his head slowly to the side and glancing at the woman dressed in a short-skirted sunsuit, turned his head quickly into the grass again and pressed his body to the earth.

'It's all right, I tell you. She'll know if you should go to hospital or not.'

Joe's body made a movement of burrowing, then he said, 'Give me me clothes.'

'Don't be silly.' The voice was gentle but brisk, and the woman, kneeling down by him, turned him over, and he, still too shaken to resist, was once again on his back. Her hands did not touch him and a silence fell on them, and then she swallowed once before saying, 'Why did they do this? Do you know them?'

Joe's head moved once from side to side. He said again, 'Me clothes,' and this time added with a beseeching note, 'please.'

As the man and woman helped Joe to his feet Brid looked away, looked out towards the sea. She knew that Joe did not want her to look at him. She had a nice picture of the sea framed in between the boles of the trees. On the horizon right at the top of the picture was a speck she knew to be a ship. She wished she was on that ship, far away from this place. Far away from everybody in it. But not everybody . . . Joe. She didn't want to be far away from Joe. Her father had said to her, 'You move out of this house the day and I'll skin you alive.' That was when she had gone down to dinner. After dinner she had gone upstairs and got her bathing costume and put it in the fancy basket with a towel. She had not cared then whether or not her father came out of the front room, for she had suddenly stopped being afraid of him. Lying in bed that morning she had faced the fact that all the wanting in the world wouldn't make him her father. He wasn't her father, and she had always known he wasn't her father. That's where the trouble had lain, and still lay; he wasn't her father. She had known that if she met him on the stairs, or in the kitchen, and he tried to carry out his threat she would fight him, tooth and nail; she would fight him to get out and go swimming with Joe Lloyd. He had been sulking in the front room when she came downstairs. Her mother had been in the kitchen when she passed through and she had said no word to detain her, and Brid knew that in defying the man she called father she was scoring one against him for her mother.

As she had hurried along the road towards the beach she had thought, I'm seventeen and if I wanted to marry, I could; he couldn't stop me. Joe likes me, he does, and I like him. I do, I do. I've never met anybody I like as I like him. He's different. Not nasty. He could never be nasty. Not even when . . . Her thoughts had skipped away from the subject and she had covered some distance before she had said to herself, 'What if he's only being nice and not serious?' And there had come a longing in her, a prayerful longing that Joe Lloyd would be serious, for she saw in his seriousness a means of escape. She would stay at home for ever and ever, as bad as it was, rather than marry *anybody*; yes, rather than marry anybody. Then she had scrambled down to the beach and up the bank towards the trees . . . and she had seen Joe.

He had looked terrible. Without being told, she had

known who had done this thing. Yet her mind would persist in ignoring his name. She could not even think of the name 'Sandy Palmer'; it was as if he didn't exist. But there were those who did exist, and they were her mother and father and her Uncle John.

The woman's voice came to her now, saying, 'Come and sit down,' and she was surprised when she turned to see them all sitting down, the man and the woman one on each side of Joe. Slowly she went and sat down opposite Joe but did not look at him, nor he at her. The man was saying, 'Now take my advice and go to the police. If they can do this once they'll do it again. They've only to get a taste for this kind of business, for anything abnormal, and they are away. You say you know who they were. What's their names? Tell me; perhaps I know them.'

Joe lowered his head still further. If he were to say Sandy Palmer the man would say, 'But why did he do it?' And could he say to him, 'He did it because he thought I was out all night with her, with Brid, when we only met at four o'clock.' And then the man would say, 'Four o'clock! Four o'clock this morning? But why did you want to meet at four o'clock this morning?' To see the dawn. It sounded funny now, daft, even improper, to ask a girl out at four o'clock in the morning. They would reckon that things could happen at four o'clock in the morning the same as they did at ten o'clock at night. Sandy Palmer had thought that . . . Sandy Palmer. He would get Sandy Palmer, and by God he would leave his mark on Sandy Palmer. Not in the same place as Sandy Palmer had left it on him. No, he wasn't that putrid. He could never stoop to that, but, by God in heaven! he would give Sandy Palmer something he would carry to his dying day, he would that.

'It was Sandy Palmer.' Brid suddenly blurted out the name, her head and chest bouncing forward as if she were being prodded in the back.

Swiftly, Joe lifted his head to look straight into Brid's eyes: it was as if she had spoken his thoughts aloud. He saw that she was still terrified. This was a new side to Brid. He hadn't had much time to find the sides to her, but this one he judged was part of her make-up; this fear-filled side came over in the trembling of her voice as she mentioned the name Sandy Palmer, and before he could say anything the man took it up, his voice hard.

'Sandy Palmer? Well, one needn't be surprised any more. Sandy Palmer . . . I know Sandy Palmer. How did you come foul of Sandy Palmer?' But without waiting for an answer the man went on, 'Was it at Telford Road school? He went there, didn't he? I had him before that.' Leonard Morley stopped abruptly. His mind having groped back, he actually knew now the first time he had thought of boys as bastards. Sandy Palmer could only have been about eleven at the time.

He remembered Sandy Palmer. Oh yes, by God! he did. For Sandy Palmer had left his mark on him, in a way, as well as on this boy. He hadn't been long at the Bodden Moor School; it was his third move since the war and he was unsettled. He remembered realising very quickly that a number of the boys at this school were tough lads. Sandy Palmer was one of them. Each had the same habit of filling the classroom with the gases from his body. They did it purposely, methodically, orderly, in rotation. To them, it was a belly-aching laughter game. Their faces would be tight with unexploded laughter. Their eyes round and bright, their nostrils would quiver as they sniffed the polluted air, and they would all be looking at him fixedly, their eyes, saying, 'What now, chum?' He should have had more sense than talk to them about this sort of thing. He had had enough experience to know that he should have got the ringleader on one side without witnesses and boxed his blasted ears, given him a kick in the backside, or shaken him until his teeth rattled, all metaphorically speaking; but no, he had had to address the whole form; and it was no other than Sandy Palmer who had run across the playground, right past the common-room window, yelling, 'What d'you think? Old Morley gave us a lesson on fartin'.' That was the day he acquired the name of Farty Morley.

He hated the nickname, loathed it. It made him curl

up inside. Sandy Palmer had left the school when he was twelve, but the nickname had stuck.

At this moment Leonard Morley was hating Sandy Palmer more than was Joe. Joe's mind was muzzy, but the man's, in the main, seemed to be clear with a hard clearness, polished with years of classroom restraint; but with a section cut off as if by a thick plate-glass window behind which his turbulent thoughts were allowed to boil. He had a longing for Sandy Palmer to return. He could see himself rolling on the ground, pounding his fists into Sandy Palmer's face, beating out of him not only the humiliation that the nickname had carried, but all the nerve-stretching, mind-explosive irritations of all the little bastards he had been forced to suffer.

The words 'Come on! Come on! snap out of it,' being briskly spoken by the woman to her husband, startled Brid somehow, for the action that had accompanied them, the tapping of the man imperiously on the arm, reminded her of a scene in the kitchen at home with her mother saying, 'Come on! Come on! snap out of it. Get going. Snap out of it.' This scene on top of the cliff had taken on a semblance of home. She didn't know this man and woman from Adam, yet it was as if she had been with them for years.

Now turning, first to Brid, then to Joe, the woman said, 'Look, we'll go down and get our things, we've got a little stove. We'll bring everything up here and make a cup of tea, eh?' And Brid looked to see Joe's reaction, and when he acknowledged the words with small jerks of his head, Brid followed suit.

'All right. Fine. That's a good idea.' The man was on his feet. He was smiling slightly and was looking somewhat boyish. He too looked from Brid to Joe and his voice took on a light note as he said, 'And then we'll all go in and have a dip. A dip won't do him any harm, will it?' He had turned to his wife, questioning, but quickly returned to Joe, saying, 'That's what you came for, isn't it, a dip?' With a swift body movement he was down on his hunkers, his face level with Joe's, and speaking low and earnestly now, with bitterness threading the words, he said, 'Go in and have your dip. Keep to your purpose; don't let them budge you an inch. If you came here to swim, swim. If you allow swine like Palmer and his gang to deviate you one inch, they've won. You've got to go on and do what you want to do in spite of them. Go right through them. D'you understand?'

Joe's head had been slightly drooped, but now he was looking at the man eye to eye. The fellow was right. If you let them frighten you, you were finished. If he remained frightened now he would never see Brid again. He could see himself avoiding this beach, avoiding the club and George's; in fact moving away altogether, just because of Sandy Palmer and what he would do next. No, the man was right. 'Go through them,' he had said, and that's what he would do. He could see his future actions clearly, he could see them reflected in the man's eyes. He would get Ossie to go with him. Yes, he would ask Ossie to go with him. He would go to the house, Sandy Palmer's house, and say, 'Look, I could have gone to the police. I could have had you locked up for what you did to me. But come on, we'll fight it out. You bring one of your chaps, I've got mine.' And they would go to some place on the fells. The light he was seeing in the man's eyes seemed to dim, and with it his heroic action of having it out with Sandy Palmer the clean way. No. It couldn't be like that; that was the way things were at one time, the way his dad would have done it, but you could not do it now. If he beat Sandy Palmer, Sandy Palmer would catch him one dark night and he'd have his pals with him. They would waylay him and beat him up. He knew the procedure; it had happened to other blokes. He had heard about them now and again in the club, and yet that club was supposed to be a good club where things like that didn't happen, because no louts or beats were allowed in.

The man said, 'What about it?'

Joe sighed, then looked at Brid. She still had that frightened look on her face. He wanted to put his hand out past the man and grip hers and say, 'Don't worry. Just let them try anything again, just let them.' He wanted to say things to her that would take that look off her face. It was an awful look. Perhaps the man was right. If they went in and had a swim it might make things normal again, it might make her look less frightened. 'All right,' he answered, 'as you say.'

'That's it.' The man got to his feet, and as he was straightening up Joe's head came up quickly and the words tumbled out of him: 'I can't. Well . . . you see . . . me trunks.' He pointed to the ground where his trunks lay, the elastic band still supporting the ripped material. Then the woman, going and picking them up, said, 'Oh, I'll soon fix these. I haven't any needle and thread with me but I've a packet of tiny safety pins in my bag. We'll do a botching job. Wait till we come back; we won't be a minute.' She turned and ran towards the top of the clearing, and the man, after one look which he divided again between Brid and Joe, ran after her.

They were alone with a matter of three feet separating them. They did not look at each other but purposely watched the man and woman running. They watched them until they had dropped over the steep bank; and they both continued to look in that direction for quite some time after the couple had disappeared. Joe would have liked to lie back and just let his body relax. It was paining again. The pain had eased off a while ago but now it was back, the skin cut on his stomach was stinging and the burn seemed worse than ever. He wished he could look at

it, examine it. What if it didn't heal and spread . . .
He turned quickly towards Brid and said softly, 'I'm
sorry for all this.'

'What?' The word sounded inane. She had looked
slightly stupid as she spoke it; and she said again,
'What?' But now it didn't sound stupid to him, for
it said, Why should he say he is sorry? Look what
has happened to him.

'It's all because of me.'

'Don't take it like that. Don't look at it like that.
He would have got at me for something else.'

'He'll not let up. I'll have to . . . I mean I won't
have to—'

He didn't let her finish. The man had said, 'Go right
through them, don't be diverted,' and so he interrupted
her with rather more conviction than he felt.

'You won't have to do anything of the sort,' he
said. 'You mean that you'll stop seeing me, don't
you? Well, that's what he wants, and he won't get
that satisfaction. You're going to go on seeing me . . .
aren't you?'

He really didn't want to be bothered talking like
this, not at the moment; he wanted to lie down and
rest, just rest. He felt sort of weak all over, shaken,
like he'd never felt even during his worst moments in
the pit. In this case, the shaking wasn't only in his
body and his mind, it seemed to have gone deeper.
He couldn't quite make it out. He told himself that

his head was too muzzy to think, but he said to Brid, in a voice that he tried to make masterful, 'The man said we came here to bathe and we did, didn't we? And that's what we'll do. We'll act as if nothing had happened.'

He turned slightly away and leaned rather heavily on his elbow. My God, that was a daft thing to say, even in an effort to take that look off her face. Act as if nothing had happened. That was wishful thinking all right, for he knew that when this muzziness left his mind his thoughts would be like those that had filled him during the moments of his ordeal; things would scream at him. Questions would scream at him; life would scream at him, life peopled with fellows like Sandy Palmer. And the main question would be: why were fellows like him allowed to get away with things? Short of murder, they got by.

By twisting round and leaning towards him, Brid brought his attention back to herself. She had one leg under her, and her hands flat on the ground supported her as she leaned forward. Her face looked even whiter than it had done before; she was looking scared beyond reason and she said, 'There's something I've got to tell you. There's something you should know. It's about . . . about what's happened, connected with it, like. It's about Sandy Palmer.'

He felt the pain of the burn lessen, he felt his whole body go cool, even take on a degree of coldness, as if he had been pushed momentarily into an ice-box. She wanted to tell him something about Sandy Palmer. Had she and Sandy Palmer . . .? Before he could stop himself he was saying in a low and agonised voice, 'You haven't been with him, have you . . . not Palmer?'

Her arms lifting quickly from the ground arched her body as if she were about to execute a backwards somersault. 'Me been with him! Me? No! No! Not that!'

He was out of the ice-box and his body began to burn again. Nothing mattered, nothing. If that wasn't the case, nothing mattered. He could stand anything but that, anything. He didn't think he could have stood that, he didn't. No, he didn't . . . Aw, well . . .

She was saying now, 'You see it's like this. His father—' Her head moved downwards, she couldn't say it.

He put out his hand towards her. 'What is it? I don't mind anything.' And he didn't. Nothing she could tell him would shake him so long as she hadn't been with Sandy Palmer. He said, 'You're frightened about something, not only this the day. What is it?' He remembered the odd way she had spoken of Palmer only a few hours ago, but now she was talking about Sandy Palmer's father.

She said in a whisper that he could only just hear, 'My mother and his father—' But she couldn't go on, she couldn't say, Sandy Palmer's father is my father, I'm his half-sister; she didn't want to admit that anything that was in Sandy Palmer was in her. At this moment, it was this thought that was terrifying her as much as anything else: that in a way she was part of Sandy Palmer, the same Sandy Palmer who had tied Joe in that way to the trees, who had stripped him naked and burnt him on . . . and burnt him on the . . . She gulped on her thoughts again and her head drooped further, and Joe's hands squeezed hers as he said, 'Look, Brid; it doesn't matter to me what your mother's done, or Palmer's father. They are nothing. Look, it's just us. Don't you realise that? It's just us.' Things were galloping much faster than they should have done. He knew where he stood in relation to her, but nevertheless things should have been taken in stages with a sort of . . . well . . . wonder. But now the pace was being forced and there was no wonder in it.

Her head was still down, and she muttered, 'It isn't only that. I . . . must tell you—'

'Well, here we are!' The woman's voice came from the brow of the slope, and when she fell forward on to the ground from a too forceful push from her husband she laughed as the things spilled out of her arms, and she called across to Brid, 'Come and give me a hand, will you?'

Brid rose slowly to her feet. She was feeling stiff and tired and yet relieved, as if she had been saved from disaster. Yet she knew the relief to be only temporary, for Joe would have to know sooner or later.

'All this paraphernalia,' the man Morley said. 'We seem to move house every weekend. The car's like a covered wagon . . . There now!' He dumped his armful of utensils and clothes almost at Joe's feet and jocularly said to him, 'Take on a bet? How many minutes before you get a cup of tea, eh?'

Joe did not respond to the jauntiness; he could not, but just moved aside and the man said, 'Five minutes from now,' and then like an agitated ant he began darting here and there, picking out things, erecting this, discarding that, while his wife smiled tolerantly at his antics as if at a child showing off.

Phyllis Morley loved her husband because she understood him. Up to a point, she guided and ruled him . . . but only up to a point. Her mother had said to her the night before she married, 'If you remember that all men are little boys you'll get along all right.' After nursing men during the war she knew all about the little boy side of them, but it wasn't the same little boy side as her mother and those like her prattled on about. She knew that the juvenile side was really a handicap, something that put a spoke into their maturity. The side that wanted to lash out with fists when their tongues would have been more effective, the little boy side that could shy away from responsibility. At one time, the teacher had taken the load, then the mother; only then came the turn of the wife. But what happened when the little boy became the teacher and the bulwark for other little boys? A war was bound to break out. Her Len was a good man, and a good teacher . . . A good teacher had to like boys, and he had liked them . . . up till then? She couldn't remember the exact date, but she could remember the name Sandy Palmer. It was from the time she first heard this name that Len's nights became restless, when he would shout out in his sleep. And she had never heard him use a really heavy word until then. She did not know all the ins and outs concerning the trouble Len had had with this boy, but she did know that he was never the same from then on. His temper became brittle, his nerves taut. It was because of this that she insisted they spend every available minute of his free time in the open, walking or swimming. When it was fine, like today, they would come down to the beach before breakfast and make a day of it. Len was always better afterwards, at least for a time. She wanted to feel resentful about the intrusion of this hated name Palmer into the day, but she couldn't, for in some peculiar way she felt that what that Palmer boy had done to this boy here had helped Len, sort of given him a form of release. Here was the little boy again. Another boy had suffered at the hands of the bully and he was no longer alone. Things weren't so bad when shared. Although her husband did not realise it, he was, in a way, glad of what had happened to this lad. She could gauge this from the boisterousness of his manner. She did not like being possessed of this knowledge.

She hastily picked up Joe's trunks and began effectively to pin a seam in them.

It was almost the same moment when the man with a cry of triumph said, 'There! Water boiling. Tea mashed. What d'you think of that for smartness?' that the woman, throwing the trunks into Joe's lap, added, 'And how's that for smartness too? They look as if they are decorated with gold thread, don't they?'

'Thanks.' Joe handled the trunks, and the woman said, 'Shall we have a cup of tea before you change, or after?'

'Oh, let's have it now,' said her husband.

'Well, give it time to draw,' she said.

'Oh, I've put enough tea in to hold a knife straight up. Come on, where are those cups. D'you mind the top of the flask?'

Brid shook her head.

'There! and with two teaspoons of sugar in it.' The man handed the cup to Joe, then added, 'Oh, I didn't ask you if you took sugar, but I suppose you do.'

Joe said, 'Thanks.' He did not mention the fact that he never took sugar. It didn't matter. He put his hands round the cup and held it to his mouth. It tasted good. Different from the tea he had at home, but good, and warm. Although his body was burning again, inside he felt the need of warmth, for, somehow he didn't feel over-good.

'Have another one?'

He handed his cup to the man, and received it from him again with another 'Thanks,' and they all sat drinking in silence for quite a while. Then with a sudden bound Len Morley was on his feet again. 'Well, now!' he said; 'we don't want to wait until it's low tide, although it doesn't matter so much down in the bay. Only it means you've got to go practically to the rocks before you get out of your depth. Well, what about it? Going to get changed?'

Brid rose slowly to her feet. She didn't want to get changed, she didn't want to bathe, but as she stood undecided the woman said, 'There's a good place over here. Come on.' And she rose and walked away to the left towards a clump of bushes, and Brid followed her.

And now the man, looking down at Joe, said seriously, 'It'll do you good, you know. It's funny what the sea does to you; it seems to wash away all your troubles. At least while you're in it.' He put out a hand and patted Joe's shoulder. 'Which school did you go to?'

'Telford Road.'

'Where are you working now?'

'The pits.'

'You mustn't let what's happened affect you too much. We must have a talk. I'm a teacher. By the way, for your information, I once taught Sandy Palmer.' Their eyes met and held, and the man nodded. 'I know Sandy Palmer only too well. You must come and have tea with us one night. Bring your friend.' He looked towards where his wife and Brid had disappeared behind the bushes, and he added, 'She's nice. A nice girl, I should say. I'll give you our address before we leave. And now come on, come on up.' He helped Joe to his feet, then said, 'I'll leave you to find your own dressing-room. Can you manage by yourself?'

'Yes; yes, I can manage.' Joe's steps were rather unsteady, not drunken, but were just as if he had indulged in a few pleasurable pints. When he stood up his head felt muzzy and he shook it vigorously as he walked in the opposite direction from Brid and also towards a clump of bushes.

The patch of bush he chose screened him effectively from the clearing but only partly from the rest of the copse. It was as he pulled his shirt over his head that he heard the sound of a motor-bike stopping. It arrested the movement of his arms and he pushed his head upwards through the neck again and looked out in the direction of the road, his body now stiff and erect and for a moment painless. It was a good many seconds later when he actually pulled his shirt off and his limbs relaxed and he felt the pain again, but as he dropped his trousers on to the ground he thought, If I saw one of them now, I'd kill him.

Four

CHARLIE TALBOT HAD NOT BEEN ABLE TO GO
swimming with the gang that morning because
he had had to take a message to his granny in Morpeth.
The ride to Morpeth and back was nothing, but once
his granny opened her mouth she forgot to shut it
again, and she always yapped and yapped to keep him
till the last minute. He would have left right away and
to hell with her, but she was always good for a few bob,
even a pound or two when she was buttered up a bit,
and he had done some buttering this morning. By! aye,
he would say he had; he was in need of a few quid. He
wanted to treat the gang to something special, Sandy
and them. It was mostly Sandy he wanted to treat.
He felt that if he had some money to splash about he

might take the place of Ronnie or Clarky in Sandy's affections. Sandy, he knew, held him of no account, and Ronnie and Clarky followed his example. He was a member of the gang only on sufferance. Of this he was well aware. Perhaps this was because he didn't look tough. But he could be tough. He could make himself tough. He'd buy another knife, one of the latest, and he would bet his mother wouldn't get her hands on that one . . . His mother! He moved his head impatiently on the thought of his mother. He had given her some lip before leaving the house this morning, although he had had to run for it. 'And if you're not back in time for your dinner, I'm not keepin' it!' she had yelled. His dinner. She could keep her dinner, she knew what she could do with it. He laid the bike against the bank and moved into the trees. Perhaps they hadn't gone home yet; they might be still on the beach. Perhaps their bikes were further in the copse. Clarky had had his lamp pinched recently. There were sods who'd pinch your granny's upper plate when she was yawning. Coo! That was a good 'un. He'd have to tell Sandy that one. As he threaded his way forward his small eyes widened and brightened as he saw the slant of a bare arm above the bushes. Coo! he was lucky; they were still here. He put his hand to the hip pocket of his tight jeans to where his wallet was bulging. What would they say when he showed them this little lot? Ten quid he had now with the three pounds he had borrowed from his granny. He stretched his nose as he thought of the word borrowed. None of them had as much as this left after they paid the instalments on their bikes and this and that. He hadn't paid his instalment for a fortnight now. The thought of his mother came to him again, and he answered it with a movement of his shoulders as he went forward, saying almost aloud, 'Well, let her find out, she can only shout.' And it was as though the word was a prompt, for he shouted, 'Sandy! I've made it, Sandy. You—' He had caught sight of a naked figure through a screen of bushes to the right, and it wasn't Sandy's. Quickly he moved his head, endeavouring to get a better view; and then his mouth fell into a long wide gape . . . It was a lass with nowt on.

He was about to turn his gaze questioningly towards the bushes to the left of him where he had first thought Sandy Palmer was, when he received the shock of his short and useless life as somebody hurled himself at him, and before he could even gasp a bloke was lathering into him with his fists. As he automatically hit back in a vain effort to stave off the blows he shouted all kinds of things. 'Help! Help! Give over! What's up? Look . . . Look here a minute! Give over! will you?' And then he was rolling on the ground crying out in agony as a fist rammed into his eye. Maddened with the pain, he now tried to bring his knee up into the fella's stomach but all he could manage was to defend his face. Then, of a sudden, the fella was wrenched off him and he lay on the ground panting and looking up through narrowed vision into a face he knew. It was Joe Lloyd, the fella that had started coming to the club and George's and looked as if he was going soft on Brid Stevens. He was being held now by a man in a bathing costume.

A woman came and bent over him and helped him to his feet, and when he was upright, with his hand covering his damaged eye, he stood swaying.

Looking at Joe, who was standing taut within the man's grasp, he said between gasps, 'You'll get it for this. What's up with you? I've done nowt to you. But you'll get it for this. See if you don't.'

Joe Lloyd was struggling again in an effort to free himself from the man, who now shouted at him, 'Get yourself away and quick!' And when he didn't move, the man added, 'Unless you want some more.'

He backed a few steps, then stopped again. And looking from one to the other, he said, 'You'll get some more; the lot of you'll get some more. Don't think you'll get away with this.' But as he turned to go he looked towards the bushes, where he had seen the girl standing with nothing on; and then, in spite of the pain of his bruises and the shock that the attack had caused, he gaped again, for although he could see only a bit of her hair and face he knew he was seeing Brid Stevens. And it was revealed to him why he had been attacked. Dragging his eyes from the bushes back towards Joe again, he cried, 'You won't get off with this. Just you wait, you mad bugger!' and the words seemed to impel him to get away, and quickly, for it was obvious the man could hardly hold back Joe Lloyd.

He was trembling as he mounted the motor cycle. He could only see out of one eye. Half of his face seemed to be extending to the end of his shoulder. He touched his cheek-bone. It felt as if it were cracked, and as he opened the throttle he said, 'Wait until I tell them! Just wait!' And he glanced in the direction of the clearing before driving off . . .

Ten minutes later Mrs Talbot, looking at her son standing in the doorway, exclaimed, 'My God! You've come off. Well, I knew you would one of these days. What happened? What did you hit? Don't just stand there. My God! What a face!'

'I didn't hit nowt.'

'You didn't hit nowt? How did you get that, then? Bill!' She threw back her head and called to her husband: 'Come here and see this. This is what I've said would happen all along.'

'I tell you, Ma, I didn't hit nowt.'

When his father appeared in the doorway he again said, 'I didn't hit nowt, Dad. I went to me granny's, as you know, and I was comin' back. I got off me bike up above the bay, near the little wood, because Sandy and them—'

'Sandy and them?' His mother's head went back. 'That Sandy Palmer will lead you to no—'

'Oh, shut up! Ma, and let me tell you. And give me something for me eye. You won't shut your mouth. I haven't seen Sandy. I went to see him; I thought they were swimming. I thought I saw him behind the bushes and I went up and I saw—' He stopped, and then said more slowly, 'There was a lass behind the bushes. She had nowt on.' He watched his mother's face shrink into primness. 'And then a fella came at me. I didn't know what hit me. He knocked me to the ground and pummelled me until another bloke pulled him off. It was a fella called Joe Lloyd, and the lass was Brid Stevens from along the road.'

'Brid Stevens? D'you mean to say she was the lass with nothing on?'

'Aye; yes, she was. She was behind some bushes and she had nowt on. Neither had he.'

'And because you caught them, the fella went for you, was that it?'

'Aye. He came at me from behind. He went mad. But he won't get off with it. When I tell Sandy—'

'You say it was Brid Stevens?'

'What've I been tellin' you . . .? Dad,' he appealed to his father who had remained silent all this time – 'haven't I been tellin' her, and she keeps on. It was

Brid Stevens and this fella Joe Lloyd.' He turned back to his mother: 'Get me somethin' for me face, will you? Have you any steak? They say steak's good.'

'I've got no steak. How would I have steak on a Sunday afternoon? The meat's cooked. My God! look at the mess you're in . . . and your suit. And that Brid Stevens. This is through her, the dirty little bitch. Goin' the same road as her mother . . . Well!'

'That's enough! That's enough!' It was the first time the man had spoken, and his wife turned on him angrily now, saying, 'Oh . . . that's enough. It's the likes of her who get sympathy. Disgrace she is, and the trouble she's caused. Look at poor Olive Palmer next door. Ruined her health and everything, the carry-on has, for years.'

'That's enough, I said. It's got nothin' to do with this. He butted in on the fella and the girl, and the fella turned on him . . . Were you looking for it?'

'No; no, I wasn't. I tell you I was just lookin' for Sandy and this fella came at me. And I wouldn't have been lookin' for it; you just have to go on the beach if you want to see that.'

'Keep your voice down.' The father looked at his son, whom he didn't like. The boy was a weak-kneed, dim, little ignoramus, and a sneaking, light-fingered liar into the bargain, whose one desire in life was to be like that lout of a Palmer next door. Bill Talbot wondered, and not for the first time, how children could be so different from their parents. He hadn't much time for John Palmer and his carrying on with Alice Stevens, but the man didn't seem to be of the type to breed a Sandy Palmer, nor did Olive Palmer seem the kind of woman to breed such a son. Funny things happened with offspring. He would have wished to have been able to say there was something of himself in his son, but look what he had been saddled with. His lad was eighteen and he was no good. No good whatsoever. He shuddered to think what he would be like at twenty-eight.

He said now, 'Well, a black eye won't kill you.' Then his attention was brought sharply from his son to his wife as she stood taking off her apron. He watched her smoothing down her hair with quick strokes of her fingers before he asked, 'Where d'you think you're goin'?'

'I'm going along to the Stevenses'.'

'What for?'

'What for? You've got to ask what for and his face like that! I don't know this Joe Lloyd, but I know Brid Stevens, and anyone with any sense knows why he got his face, 'cos he saw her when he shouldn't have seen her.'

'Now look here, you're not—'

'You can talk as much as you like. You've never done anything in your life for him but criticise him, and I don't expect you to defend him. Well, that may be your way of looking at things, but it isn't mine. I'm goin' along to the Stevenses'.'

Bill Talbot rested one hand on the table, the other he rubbed across his mouth. It was no good and he knew it. He could stop her going to the Stevenses'. Yes he could stop her by force: he could push her into the room and give her a clout, and it wouldn't be the first time. But when he was at work he couldn't stop her from doing what she wanted to do. If she didn't go to the Stevenses' now, she would go the minute he went out of the house . . . He turned and went back into the front room and took up the paper.

'Come on.'

'Aw! Ma.'

'Never mind aw Ma'ing me. Come on, I say.'

'Look Ma; I'll see Sandy—'

'You'll see Sandy when I'm finished with you. Come on.'

'What about somethin' on me eye?'

'I'll see about that later. Come on, it'll keep.' She yanked him by the upper arm across the kitchen and out of the back door and down the long back garden. As they reached the gate a voice from the next garden said, 'Anything wrong, Mrs Talbot?'

Olive Palmer had always addressed her neighbour as Mrs Talbot. She was of the opinion that her family were a cut above the Talbots, and she imagined she made this evident by never resorting to Christian names. Christian names made for familiarity. From her seat behind the glass porch adjoining the scullery she had heard the Talbots going at it, and now she rose from the deck-chair and looked down the garden towards where the mother and son waited.

'It's that Brid Stevens. Charlie here was going looking for your Sandy, when he was attacked by a fella, all because of Brid Stevens.' Mrs Talbot was well aware of Mrs Palmer's condescending attitude, and her own retribution took the form of pity and vindictiveness; what affected Brid Stevens affected John Palmer . . . and so on.

'Brid?' Mrs Palmer was slowly advancing down the garden, and she said again, 'Brid?' And now the two women were facing each other close over the fence, and Mrs Talbot gave the rest of her information in tones which were low and hushed, as the subject warranted. 'She was up there in the wood naked, so my Charlie says. He came on them, and this fella went for him. Just look at his face.'

Mrs Palmer looked at Charlie Talbot's face and her body began to quiver, though not noticeably. She said again, 'Brid?' and added, 'like that?' And Mrs Talbot made a slight obeisance with her head before pushing Charlie forward and moving away.

Olive Palmer returned up the garden path more quickly than she had come down it. Her walk was even spritely, and this was rather surprising, for she was a semi-invalid, carrying in her body aches and pains which were the symptoms of no known disease. Yet they were there and gave, from time to time, evidence of their presence by sending her heart into a panic of beats and her nerves to screaming pitch. When she reached the kitchen her husband was putting the last of the dinner dishes away. He had washed up as he always did on a Sunday, and every other day, for that matter. The dishes were always in the sink to greet him on his return from work, but this did not disturb him.

John Palmer's disposition was such that he could take the chores of housework in his stride. He was at heart a kindly man, aiming to hurt no-one, but nevertheless hurting, through weakness, all those people who touched on his life.

He turned at the unusual sound of his wife's quick step. He had a side dish in one hand and a tea towel in the other, and with a not unusual feeling of apprehension he waited for her to speak. But she stared at him for a full minute before saying, 'There's trouble up there.'

The words were ordinary enough, and it wasn't the first time he had heard her utter similar ones, but he could see now she was excited about something, even pleased. He knew every phase of his wife's reactions to practically every situation and he knew that whatever the trouble was now, it was bad. He had never heard her walk so briskly or look so bright for a long time.

John Palmer never criticised his wife, even to himself; he knew that for whatever had happened to her he was to blame, and he remembered that she hadn't always been like this. At one time she had been lively and pleasant. If the war had not brought him and Tom Stevens together again and renewed their boyhood friendship, and if Alice Stevens had been a different woman from what she was, things between them might have been different. If only Tom had attempted to prove, back at the beginning, that Brid was not his, things would have come to a head and been finished with. But apparently Tom couldn't bring himself to do it. He likely fooled himself that women were known to be a few weeks over their time. It was not unusual. And if only Alice had been a bit decent to him and not treated him like a mucky rag; after all, she lived in the same house and took his money.

The first time he had refused to leave Olive and the two youngsters and go off with her, Alice had threatened to go off on her own and leave both him and Tom high and dry. And since that day she had repeated the plea and the threat at least twice a year. But she had never been able to carry out the threat. She wanted him as much as he wanted her. That was the funny thing about this business, John Palmer thought: that he could have principles which tied him to his wife and children, yet he could still go on taking his pal's wife whenever he had the chance. It was this facet of his life that made a mockery of decency and troubled him not a little. Even now, when the desire for Alice nearly drove him up the wall and the solution would be to do as she had always wanted, go off with her – there were no young bairns to think about now – he just couldn't bring himself to do it. He had only to look at Olive and see what he had reduced her to, and that would be enough. He put down the side dish and said, 'What's the trouble? How d'you know?'

'It's Brid. Mrs Talbot's just dragged their Charlie along to them. His face is all knocked about. He said a fella hit him because he came upon them, this fella and Brid, in the copse above the bay near Stockwell Hill.' She now lowered her eyes demurely and delivered the barb: 'Brid had nothing on, he said.'

'What! nothing on? I don't believe it. Brid? I know what Charlie Talbot is, he's a little rat of a thing, is Charlie Talbot.'

Olive Palmer saw that her husband was angry, agitated and angry, and hurt, and she wanted him to be hurt. She watched him roll down his sleeves, then go to the back of the door and take down his old coat.

'Where are you going?'

'Where d'you think?' His tone was unusually sharp, to her, that is.

As he passed her, Olive Palmer warned herself to

say nothing: if he knew her reactions she also certainly knew his. With this knowledge she had kept him where she wanted him for years. She had experienced all she wanted of one side of married life long before Sandy was born. Her husband's affair with Alice Stevens had broken her up, but rather from the fear of losing the security that a nice home and a regular pay packet ensured than of losing the love of her man. She hated Alice Stevens, but more so did she hate her daughter Brid. Not only because she knew without a shadow of doubt that her husband was Brid's father, but because of the fear that had grown in her these last few years that their Sandy was getting sweet on her. The only thing that had stopped her from telling her son the truth was the fact that he would be nearly sure to turn on his father, and if things were dragged into the open there was no knowing what John might do. He might, even at this stage, walk out on her – there were no children to hold him now and Alice Stevens was always ready and waiting.

She picked up the tea towel that had dropped to the floor, and as she was about to hang it on the rack near the stove, Sandy appeared in the kitchen doorway. 'I'm off,' he said.

'Sandy!' She had her back to him.

'Aye?'

'There's trouble down below. Your Dad's just gone along.'

'Trouble? What kind of trouble?' Sandy was standing stiffly with his hands by his side, his eyes narrowed. He was staring at the back of his mother's head and she still didn't turn to him as she spoke.

'It's to do with Brid. Apparently she's been sportin' in the copse above the bay with some fella and Charlie Talbot saw them. He was looking for you.'

'Sportin'?' The sparse flesh on his face moved into furrows as he repeated the word. The questioning tone he had used made her reply defensive.

'Well, what else would you call it, her running around up there stark naked?'

'Brid? Nak—' He did not finish but stared at his mother as she turned towards him.

'Well, I don't know how far it's true. You know as much as me, but that's what Charlie Talbot came back and said, and he's brought his face to prove it. You should see it. He's along there now with his mother.'

She watched her son's eyes drop away from hers. She did not care if Brid Stevens ran around stark naked with the whole of South Scardyke so long as it wasn't with her son. She saw the fury behind the tightness of his face and it confirmed her opinion of his feelings for Brid Stevens. She felt sick. Pray God this business today would put the damper on it. She watched him spin about and run along the passage, and then she heard the front door bang, to be followed almost immediately by the faint click from the garden gate. He must have taken the path in a couple of leaps.

'All right, Mrs Talbot. All right.' Tom Stevens was speaking in a quiet way, a toneless quiet way. 'You've had your say and Charlie's had a beatin' up. Well, you're not going to hold me responsible for that, are you? And don't say again—' he held up his hand almost in front of her face— 'and don't say again that it's Brid's fault. When I see all you've said I'll believe it, and not until.'

'You think he's a liar then, you think she wouldn't do it?'

'I'm sayin' nowt until I see her.'

After the scene of the morning Tom Stevens seemed strangely calm. He moved now towards the back door and, opening it, indicated that he wished Mrs Talbot and her son to leave. And Mrs Talbot, pushing Charlie out in the same way as she had pushed him in, said, 'Of course, you won't want to believe it. That's natural, I grant you. But something's goin' to be done about this, an' I can tell you straight I'm goin' to report that fella to the police, and you won't be able to hush things up then.' She looked around the assembled company from Tom Stevens to Alice Stevens, and then to the corner of the triangle, as she thought of him, John Palmer, and said plainly, 'There's been too much hushin' up, if you ask me.'

'Aw, come on, Ma. Come on out of it.' Charlie's voice pulled her after him.

Tom Stevens closed the door quietly on the pair, and then with the knob in his hand he stood looking at it for a moment before turning to face his wife and his pal. It was a different Tom Stevens now, entirely different from the one who had just denied Brid's lapse to Mrs Talbot, for, after staring first at his wife and then at his pal, then back to his wife again, he brought out between stiffened jaws, 'Nice set up, isn't it, eh? Playin' games in the wood stark naked. That's for you, eh?'

'I don't believe it, Tom, and you shouldn't either.' John Palmer's voice was quiet, and he was startled at the bellow that answered him.

'No! you wouldn't believe it. No! of course you wouldn't, not you. But I do. I believe it all right, and I've got good reason to believe it.' His gaze swung to his wife, and his voice dropping slightly, he said again, 'Runnin' round naked in the wood. By God! I hope she's still naked when I get me hands on her; I'll take the skin from her ribs, you see if I don't.'

As he dived across the kitchen, pulling at his shirt collar to bring the ends together, Alice Stevens found her voice and in a high squeak demanded, 'Where're you goin'?'

'Where d'you think?' He had unfolded his collar and was dragging a tie round his neck now. 'Where d'you think? I said she hadn't to go out, didn't I? I said what I'd do if she did, didn't I? Well, I'm going up there to see the fun and games and add me quota to them. That's where I'm going . . . MRS STEVENS!'

'No, you're not. Oh, no you're not. By God! you're not.' She was standing in front of him. They seemed to have forgotten the presence of John Palmer.

'You try an' stop me. Just try and stop me. Try and stop me hammering her. If I don't do it the day I'll do it the morrow. She's been askin' for something big for a long time and by God she's going to get it. I'll let her see if she can shame me. Runnin' round naked. By God! I will. I'll let her see; you wait. You wait, just wait.'

'She wouldn't do that, not Brid. Have some sense you silly, dim bugger.'

'Silly, dim bugger, am I? Silly dim bugger.' His face had turned a pasty grey and his upper set of false teeth moved in unison as he ground his lower teeth against them. 'Aye, I'll have some sense. After all these years, I'll have some sense. You'll see what sense I'll have.'

He was nodding in emphasis at her when John Palmer spoke in a voice different from that which either of them had heard before: there was no laughter in it, no jocular tone, no placating, no quiet reasoning, but a definite quality of authority: it stated his right to have a say in what was to happen to Brid. He said, 'You won't touch her. You won't lay a hand on her.'

'I won't, eh?' Tom Stevens had turned and was

eyeing his life-long pal, and he repeated again, 'I won't eh?' and John said, 'You won't, Tom. You won't now or at any time. We'll have this out later, but at this minute I'm going to—' He was stopped by a knock on the back door and at the same time it was pushed open and his son entered, his whole attitude trigger-sprung for trouble. But he didn't give his son time to open his mouth; instead, he demanded in a voice of strange authority, 'You got your bike out back?'

Sandy nodded sharply before saying, 'What's this I hear—?'

'Never you mind what you've heard. Get the bike going and come on. Take me to Stockwell Hill.'

Sandy remained rigid. There was nothing more he wanted than to go to Stockwell Hill and see Brid caught red-handed at something or other. Yet he felt he'd be too late for that now, and his sharp wits told him that if he went to the hill and that bloke was there and he spilled the beans there might be trouble. But his Dad was acting different, not easy goin' and laughin' any more. When he was pushed through the door he wrenched his shoulder from his father's grasp and snapped, 'Give over! Who you pushin' about?'

'I'll let you know that an' all later. Meantime, get that bike goin', and quick.'

As he growled this order at his son, Tom Stevens's voice came yelling after him, 'We'll see who's goin'

to deal with this. Who the hell d'you think you are?
Don't forget I've still got me rights. Don't try to take
them an' all off me or you'll be in for something, mind.
Worms turn, you know, worms turn. You mind your
own damn business; this is my business and I'll see to
it, and her. You'll bloody well see I will, at that.'

When he heard the sound of the motor-bike starting
up he was dragging his coat on, and he turned to Alice
where she was standing near the window, her hand
across her mouth, and he shouted at her, 'Nice thing
this, isn't it, eh? Nice thing. One thing after the other
over the years I've been stripped of, through you and
him. Well, this is the showdown, Alice, me girl, this
is the showdown. As he said, we'll talk later, and
by God we will an' all. But he's not playing God
Almighty in this business; I've brought her up and
to all intents and purposes she's mine . . . mine!' He
was now standing close behind Alice, and he dug his
forefinger between her ribs so forcibly that her head
jerked. But she didn't move, nor did she speak. 'I've
brought her up, haven't I? To all intents and purposes
I'm her father. Aren't I her father? Go on, tell me I'm
her father.' He waited, and when she made no answer
he went on, 'Well then, I'll act like her father.'

There came another dig between her ribs, and on
this Alice Stevens turned and dashed to the table. She
grabbed a knife by the handle, and gripping it in her
fist and pointing the blade towards him, she growled,

'Get out! Get out while you're able or by God I'll ram this in you. You sod! I will, mind . . . I will.'

Slowly he backed a few steps from her. He was checked and evidently a little frightened, but he laughed and said, 'You would like to, wouldn't you? Go on then, why don't you do it?' For a moment longer he watched the knife trembling in her fist, then he turned on his heel and went out.

When the door closed on him she dropped the knife onto the table, then put her hands to her head for a while before running upstairs and pulling some shoes from the bottom of the cupboard and a coat from the wardrobe. She was pushing her arms into the coat as she ran down the stairs again. Once out of the house, she slowed her running to a quick walk down the road towards Furness's Garage. She couldn't wait for a bus, there wasn't time, and anyway they ran oddly on a Sunday. She would have to get a taxi out to Stockwell Hill before he got there.

'If he wasn't one of them, there wasn't much sense in it, was there? You shouldn't take it out on Peter for what Paul has done.'

The teacher knew that if he had been in Joe's place he would have done the same thing, but he couldn't get over the habit of moralising.

Joe was sitting on the ground again and he was panting, but he said in angry tones, 'He was one of them; I know him. He's always trailing after them. They likely sent him back to see what was going on. Or if I'd skedaddled or not. Or perhaps to see if you had gone' – he jerked his head at the teacher – 'so they could come back and try on some of their games.'

'No; no, I don't think he came for that. In fact, I think I heard him call out Sandy Palmer's name.'

'Yes, he called out all right, but that could be a blind. You don't know that lot.'

The teacher gave a twisted smile and said with a touch of authority in his voice, 'I know them. I knew them before you were born.'

Joe's head drooped, and he swung it slowly from side to side, biting on his lip as he did so, and when he stopped he asked quietly, 'Do you think he'll bring them back?'

'There's no knowing what he'll do, but I shouldn't worry. If they come back there's always the police to deal with them. You would have let them deal with the matter in the first place if you had taken my advice. But there, come on; are we going in the water or not?'

Joe looked from the man to the woman and then to Brid and back to the man again. The man, he thought, seemed to be running things and he didn't know now whether he liked it or not. He could recognise in him the teacher, ordering, organising, setting a kind of life pattern. He supposed the man had done this so often that he couldn't get out of it. If he hadn't felt so worked up and worried, and his body hadn't felt so painful and his head so muzzy, he thought that he might have answered, 'If you want to go in, go in. Leave us be, will you?' yet at the same time he felt that he owed this man and woman something, and it made him rise to his feet.

The woman now laughed and said, 'The pins held, anyway.' Then, in the manner of a young girl, which did not suit either her figure or her age, she ran with a leaping movement towards the bank top, and the man, after dividing a smile between Joe and Brid, followed her, but more slowly.

Joe now looked at Brid. Her face was even whiter than it had been, if that were possible. It was so white he was forced to say, 'Don't worry, they won't try anything on. As the man says, if they do we'll get the polis. Come on.' He half extended his hand towards her.

She didn't take it, or move, but she said, 'I'm frightened, Joe. Charlie Talbot's spiteful; he could bring them back, as you said.'

He moved closer to her and was about to deny the assumption, which he felt in his own mind was really inevitable, when his glance was caught by the discoloured mark on her neck. It was a disjointed mark, stopping and starting over a patch of about six inches, dark blue in the middle and red at the ends. The red spread down to the strap of her bathing costume.

He brought his eyes up towards her face and he said quietly, 'That's fresh.'

'It's nothing.' She hitched the strap carelessly over the mark as if to demonstrate that it caused her no pain.

'Who did it?'

'I . . . I . . .' She jerked her head rapidly and brought out, 'I fell against the bed-post.'

'That's not good enough. Who did that?' He lifted his finger and pointed to her neck.

'Joe—' she was looking into his face, 'I've got to talk to you. I've got to talk to somebody. It's about me father. We'll talk after . . . Look, let's go and have that swim now. They'll only come back for us. They're trying to be kind. They're nice. Let's go.'

'All right, all right. Have it your own way.' His body, for the moment, seemed to reclaim its old strength. The fact that she was evidently frightened, that someone had hit her and that she wanted to talk about her father made him in some odd way feel old, and responsible; her need of him was like a salve on the humiliations of this past hour. He said, 'All right, but we won't stay in long, 'cos me mother's expecting us home to tea.'

'Me as well?'

'Of course . . . I've told her about you.'

Her lids drooped slowly, then she raised them quickly and her eyes held his with a searching look for a second. Then she turned from him and walked towards the edge of the clearing.

When they reached the bank top, the man and woman were already in the water; and when Brid waved a hand, the woman shouted, 'Hurry along! It feels grand.'

Joe helped Brid down the bank, and then they picked their way over the sand-strewn rocks to the edge of the tide.

The water felt wonderfully cool as it flowed round Joe's legs, and when it was above his knees he turned to Brid and actually smiled, saying 'It feels good, doesn't it?'

She nodded back at him, but did not answer his smile.

'How far can you swim?' he asked her.

'Not very far. The width of the baths . . . back and forth. I've never tried the length yet.'

'You can always swim further in the sea; it's the salt that keeps you up.'

He went under and when his head broke the surface again he stood up and squeezed the water from his hair. It was as the man had said, he felt better already. His body had stopped aching and the burn, after smarting unbearably for a moment, had ceased to pain him. It was as if the salt water had cauterised it; it felt healed.

Brid stood still in the water. She felt reluctant to go

further and let it cover her. She looked towards the man and woman and a section of her mind wrenched itself from the fears that were filling it and paused to deal with them. She watched them diving up and down like porpoises. They were laughing and making a lot of noise, as young people did. It was odd, she thought, them going on like that; it wasn't right somehow, for they were old. Well, they were over forty. And it was odd an' all how they had tacked themselves on to them. Yet she realised that if the man hadn't come when he did Sandy Palmer and the others would surely have come back right away. She shivered as if from the coolness of the water. Charlie Talbot would be home now. Would he tell Sandy Palmer? And would Sandy Palmer go and tell her father? No, she didn't think he would, somehow, because if there was any explaining to do there would be trouble for him all right. She looked at Joe now. He was swimming with jerky breast strokes. Joe was nice. He was more than nice. She wanted to think about Joe but her mind would not stay on him; it was back on Sandy Palmer again. Once she had started thinking of Sandy Palmer she couldn't stop. Joe, her mother and father and Uncle John were, for the moment, blotted out. What more would he have done if she hadn't come up the cliff at that minute? Eeh! God. She would never be able to get rid of the picture of Joe's stretched body. Sandy Palmer was rotten, filthy. If he came near her ever again she would scream, even if it was out in the street. She had a picture of herself clawing his face. She could see the flesh coming off in strips. Shocked at the ferocity of her thinking, her body responded and she plunged away into the water until it was almost up to her shoulders. Joe came swimming towards her, and as he straightened up and stood in front of her she noticed that his oxters weren't even covered with the water, yet their heads were on a level. They were practically of the same height. He had rather a large head, had Joe. It was a beautiful head. He had beautiful eyes too, and she liked his voice. She found she wanted to cry and her lips trembled.

'Come on. Come on.' His voice was very low and coaxing. 'Look, there's nothing to be frightened about any more. I tell you there isn't. They won't dare show up again.'

She shook her head and lowered her eyes to the miniature waves that were dancing between them.

'Is it something else that's worrying you?'

She jerked her chin to the side, almost on to her shoulder and she was looking towards the man and woman again. Side by side, they were swimming towards them, and with a deep note of irritation in her voice, she said, 'I wish they would go. I wish they would leave us alone.'

He had his back to the couple and he said, 'Aye yes, so do I. But look, we'll soon be on our way home. Come

on, have a swim for a little. It'll make you feel good. It
has me. You've no idea. I wouldn't have believed it.'

'Take the plunge!' It was the man shouting. He,
too, was standing upright now and addressing Brid.
'If you don't go right under you'll catch cold. You
shouldn't stand about even on a day like this, you
should go under. Come on, we'll race you to the
rocks. What d'you say? All of us. Let's see you do
your stuff.' His voice was loud and jovial and seemed
much larger than himself. His wife stood abreast of
him. Her short hair and face were running with
water. At this moment it resembled a boy's face, a
boy's head. She too addressed herself to Brid. 'Come
on,' she said; 'breast stroke. Can you do the breast
stroke?'

For answer, Brid, moving to the side of Joe and not
waiting for any signal, dropped passively into the water
and began to swim. The three of them watched her for a
moment. Her movements were slow and her style was
good. Then Joe was following her. Then the man and
woman, and now they were all swimming towards the
rocks that looked like a half circle of schoolboys' caps
bobbing on the horizon.

Joe turned his head to look at Brid. She was
swimming steadily, slowly. She had said she could
do only the width of the baths, but from the sureness
of her strokes he guessed she had been modest or
had compared herself with some of the top-notch

swimmers. She was a better swimmer than himself, that was sure, or the man and woman.

'We'll sit on the rocks.' It was the man calling.

When they reached the peaked black caps they hung on, one after the other. There had been no effort made to race by any of them. The man, last in grabbing at the slippery surface, shouted as if they were all miles away: 'It's going down fast. It'll show the flat ones shortly. We'll be able to lie here and sunbathe.'

Joe became irritated again. He wished the man would shut up. He always seemed to be talking. As he clung on to the rock he felt himself being forcibly swayed this way and that by the pressure of the water dragging through the rocks. When the pressure pushed him up he could see right out to the far horizon, or where he guessed it to be, for now the whole surface of the sea was a shimmering sheet of light which hurt his eyes. He looked along at Brid. She was about three yards away from him, and she too was moving up and down, and she too was looking towards the horizon. He was thinking how nice it would have been, in spite of all that had passed, if they had been here alone together. And yet he knew he should be grateful to this couple. God knows what might have happened to him if the man hadn't come along. His thoughts at this point took on the same pattern as had Brid's. They would likely have come back and started on him again and made Brid watch. Oh, he knew Sandy Palmer was capable of anything. Anything. He had heard a lot about badness, real badness. He had only to listen to the men in the pit talking during the break time. If any of the old soldiers got together it was always about the war and the things the Germans did. And the things that some of the Russians did to the Germans. But – and he had thought of this before – they never talked about what the English did to the Germans. No, they never talked about that. They talked as if they, the English, were a race without human frailties, without such reactions as bitterness, hate, and wickedness. He knew that they liked to think of themselves in that light. Decent blokes, too. He had said as much to his father once, and his father had said, 'Put a gun into any man's hand and he's no longer a human being. You've just got to see what they do to animals. Nice fellas who say they love birds and get all sentimental when they see them flying against a dawn sky. Then bang – bang! Down they come. But that's nothing to wartime, 'cos then they've a licence for killing men, and the more poor buggers on the other side they blow to hell the more applause and medals they get. In peacetime you would be locked up and hung for the things you get praise for in a war. You're a bad bugger if you kill a man without a licence. War is a funny thing, and you can take it from me, Joe, that when Johnny Hertherington and Fred Cooper start thinking back an' talkin', they are likely shutting their eyes to the things they did themselves. I was in the war and I know . . . I know. Even after the peace was signed, the things that happened . . . my God! the things that happened. It's circumstances and chance that bring out the rottenness in a man.'

Could you blame circumstances and chance for the things that were in Sandy Palmer? His dad had been wise, but could he have found an explanation for Sandy Palmer? He doubted it. Without war, without chance or circumstance, Sandy Palmer would be bad, really bad, vile. He'd make his chance. He'd make the circumstances. His mother would have said the devil was in Sandy Palmer, and my God, she could be right.

They were all quiet, all seemingly taken up with bobbing up and down and retaining their hold on the slippery cracks in the rocks. The water was making a different noise now, not just a lapping, slapping noise, but a sucking, swishing noise, deep and distant, yet near, under their feet, in fact. The tide had turned and already it was racing for freedom away from the enclosure of the bay, struggling to get between the barriers into the wider sea again.

The man felt the suction through his toes and was about to remark upon it, but as he looked along past his wife's face, her chin resting on the surface of the water, to the other two, he decided to remain quiet. He was worried a bit, more about the girl than the boy because, whereas the boy was trying to throw off his experience, she still retained that terrified expression, as if she were waiting for something similar to happen again. If she were his daughter he would be worried about her altogether. She looked all nerves, tightly strung. He was well aware that both the boy and the girl were wishing him and his wife were far away; they were not clever enough to be able to hide their feelings. Oh yes, they were civil, and even grateful that he had made his appearance when he did, but he knew that they wanted to be alone. He could leave them alone from now on, yet somehow he was reluctant to do so. He himself had had enough of the water. This was the third time he had been in in as many hours. Now he would like nothing better than to go and continue his sunbathing on the beach, but this couple seemed to have a call on him. He couldn't understand really why he felt as he did – teacher's training, he supposed. The emergency was over and he should leave them to themselves, but there was a subtle reason why he was reluctant to go. Phyllis would likely be able to put her finger on it. She was very good at being able to spot the whys and wherefors of one's actions and reactions, much better at it than he was, and yet it was he who always did the talking and explaining. He wished they could have a talk now. He would put the question whether or not what the girl saw today would have a lasting effect on her. Was she the sensitive type who wouldn't be able to forget in a hurry that slim figure stretched between the trees? He doubted it really. The modern girl was different. All the anatomical secrets of a boy were known to her even before she left school. By! yes. Her curiosity was like an acid eating through the outer covering, not resting until it laid bare the exciting stimulus beneath. She couldn't wait. There had been that case of Ridley, which must have been going on since he was ten and the girl twelve, and under everybody's nose at that. That was an odd thing about the present generation of girls. It was no new thought that women were the real hunters but they had, in other generations, covered their actions with a veil of decorum. But not the girls of today. They did the chasing openly, shamelessly. It had made him actually squirm to see an unresponsive male leaning up against a wall with a girl's stomach, breasts and thighs pressing hard at him while her hands sought to rouse him with widespread fingers stroking both sides of his face. And look at that young cow in the fifth form at the Barnes Road School, who had nearly driven Pat Bailey up the wall sitting with her legs apart whenever she got the opportunity and pulling her skirts up to show him a bit more, and never blinking when she looked at him, and saying, 'Ye ... es, sir, Mis ... ter Bailey.' They had laughed in the common-room, offering to change places with him, but it had been no laughing matter. It had been serious. So serious that

Pat had moved. He had been sorry about that, for he had liked Pat.

But about this girl here. No, he didn't think it had been the sight of her boy-friend's naked body that had shocked her so much as ... Well, what? He really didn't know. Was it this Palmer gang she was afraid of? She had looked ready to pass out when the young fellow had jumped on that interloper a few minutes back. And the look of fear hadn't eased from her face since then. He looked towards her now. She was moving from the rock to which she had been clinging to the next one, and he saw her twist herself about and up, and sit as it were on top of the water, and he called, 'Oh, you've found the flat one, then. There's another just to the side; we'll all be able to get on it in a minute or so. She's running down fast now.'

Joe did not listen to the man; at least, he paid no heed. He moved along towards Brid's legs and, looking up at her, he said, 'How did you know it was a flat one?'

'I could see it through the water. I'm ... I'm a bit tired, I think.' She made an attempt at lightness by saying, 'It's a bit wider than the baths.' She had been looking down at Joe as she spoke, and then he saw her eyes lift above his head as a voice came from the beach, and he registered immediately, with an answering tremor of fear in his stomach, the swift intensifying of the expression that had been on her face since he had first seen her this afternoon.

When he pulled his body round and trod water he could just make out the two figures on the beach, and if Sandy Palmer's outline had not been seared into his mind he would not have recognised him. For a moment, he felt sick, as if he had swallowed a mouthful of salt water, and his body began to ache again and the burn began to smart.

'Brid! . . . Brid! . . . Here a minute!' It wasn't Sandy Palmer's voice that came across the water but that of the man with him, and the teacher, now close to both Brid and Joe, said rapidly, 'That's Palmer, isn't it? Who's that with him?'

He too was treading water and he swung round to look up at Brid. She was staring towards the shore as she muttered, 'Me Uncle John . . . his father.'

'You're cousins, then?' The man's mouth remained open when he finished speaking.

'No. No.' She shook her head slowly, still looking towards the shore. 'I . . . I just call him that. They live near us.'

She looked down now and into Joe's face. She was drenched with an apprehensive fear that amounted to terror. She began gabbling to herself and it became almost audible. Oh, she wished that man and woman weren't here, then she could tell Joe.

'Brid! Brid! Come here a minute!'

'Don't go.' The man put out a hand as if she had been about to drop into the water, but she had made no motion whatever. She remained still. Rigidly still. The water was just lapping round her buttocks now and she had her hands flat on the rock on each side of her hips, pressing hard as if to support herself.

'You stay where you are. I'll go and talk to him.'

Joe wanted to put out his hand and say, 'No, you don't, this is my business. I'll deal with this. It's about Brid and me. It's our business, my business.' But he didn't, for he knew he was in no state to deal with Sandy Palmer and his father. His legs stopped their treading at the thought that if Sandy Palmer came into the water and went for him, there was no doubt but that he would get the better of him. Hold him under. He could well imagine him doing it. That business up on the cliff must have taken a lot out of him; he felt weak as if he hadn't eaten for days. Deep inside he knew that he was no match for Sandy Palmer or any of them. Yet he had lathered into Charlie Talbot. He was pleased at the memory. But that had been done on the spur of the moment, and Charlie Talbot was alone. If Sandy Palmer's father was anything like his son there would be little chance for anybody they decided to tackle. He stayed where he was and watched the teacher swimming towards the beach, and knew that the woman had moved past him and hauled herself onto the rock next to Brid. She did not touch her but just sat next to her in a similar position, with both her hands flat at her sides . . .

Sandy Palmer did not recognise the man swimming towards them; even when he stood up in the water and, with a swing of the hips, thrust his legs forward he still did not recognise him. But when he stood before them, running his hands over his head, he thought with a start, Why, it's old Farty Morley. What's he doin' with them? When the man looked at him he stared him straight back in the eye. He had taken old Farty Morley's measure at school: pap soft he was, always yapping. He had made up his mind to lead him one hell of a life but he had been moved away before he really got going. Lucky for him.

John Palmer did not know the man standing before him and he said gruffly, 'What d'you want?'

'I might ask you that.'

John screwed up his eyes and peered at the bloke. 'Who are you, anyway? I was calling to my ... to young Brid Stevens. I want her here a minute.'

'She's not coming.'

'Not coming? Look here! Who the hell are you? What business is it of yours what she does? I've never clapped eyes on you in me life afore.'

'No, you haven't, but your son here has. We know each other, don't we, Sandy?'

Sandy Palmer remained silent; only his lower jaw moved, first one way and then the other, to be thrust forward as the man continued, 'I saw your handiwork this afternoon, Sandy. I would have recognised it anywhere.'

He was speaking as a teacher now, treating him to his sarcastic form of address, calling him Sandy as if he liked him.

Sandy Palmer said not a word, but his father put in briskly, 'Look here! I don't know what you're at.'

'No, I don't think you do, Mr Palmer. I'm referring to a little game your son played on another young fellow this afternoon, just over an hour ago. Do you know he thought he was in Rome, crucifying the Christians?'

John Palmer lowered his head and stared under drawn brows at the man before him. He sounded a little bats. What had he to do with this anyway? And talking about Sandy crucifying a Christian. He darted a quick glance at his son before saying, 'Look, I don't know who you are or what you're getting at, but to me you're just talking plain daft.'

'I happen to be a teacher.' The voice now was brisk. 'I once taught your son. I was on the beach this afternoon and heard a cry. It was from the girl you call Brid. She had just reached the top of that bank' – he flung his arm dramatically sideways, his finger pointing – 'and she saw there . . . D'you know what she saw there, Mr Palmer? Just what I said, a crucifixion, or an imitation one. Your son and his pals had strung up a boy, her boy, between two trees. They had stripped him naked. And you know something else?'

'Shut your big mouth, you're daft. He's up the pole, Dad.' Sandy had advanced one step towards the man, but before he could raise his hand, as was his intention, his father's arm came across him, and John Palmer said to the man quietly, 'Go on.'

The teacher looked into John Palmer's face, which was not more than a foot from his now, and he went on. 'They had not only stripped him and stretched his limbs between two trees, but—' he paused, 'he, your son, burnt him with a cigarette . . . here.' As the teacher pointed dramatically down to himself, John Palmer, after following the man's hand, turned and looked at his son. He had no need to ask if this were true, for in his heart he knew it *was* true. He knew there was something rotten in his son, and he had feared it. Of late, he'd had a number of worrying fears about him, the main one being that he was sweet on Brid. He had lain awake at nights in a sweat and an agony over this, and would get up in the morning determined to tell him; only, when he looked into his son's face across the breakfast table, the truth would freeze in his mouth because he was afraid of the boy's reaction to this knowledge. It had been different with Harry. Harry knew, but had never turned nasty. He had never told Harry, his mother had. His son's voice was now shot at him, crying. 'All right! All right! I did it. And I'd do it again. He was out with Brid all night, wasn't he? You're supposed to like Brid, aren't you?' He dared at this point to thumb his father in the chest, and when he added, 'Concerned about Brid, aren't you? very concerned about Brid.' John Palmer knew with a shock of surprise that his son had somehow become aware of the relationship between himself and Brid.

John Palmer did not now think of himself, or of the other one who was concerned in Brid's beginnings, or of those who had suffered from her existence; but he thought of that boy stretched between two trees, naked and waiting for the cigarette end to be pressed on his privates. Christ! and his son had done that! The sweat ran out of the pores of his face, and he rubbed the back of his hand up under his cap.

'Oh, for Christ's sake don't look so bloody pi! You're as bad as this bloke. He—'

'Shut up! Shut your mouth. I'll deal with you later.' There was in his father's voice a deep threat that Sandy had not heard before. To his mind his old man had always been easy going, even a bit soft. It wasn't until that night he had talked with their Harry that he knew why he had been easy going . . . soft. He was caught, caught in a cleft stick between two women and he had to go easy. He had never been afraid of his father, despising him somewhat even before he knew of his double life, and since this knowledge had come to him he had hated him, and when he was confronted with the placidity of him he wanted to spit in his gob. But now, looking at his father, he could see no placidity; his face was changed. He had turned into someone who would strike out even before speaking, hit out as quick as look at you. He knew the type, he'd had to weigh them up. There were those who'd take it and those who wouldn't, and his old man had become one of the latter. They were staring at each other. Then his father's eyes lifted sharply towards Stockwell Hill, away above the beach, and he knew that the figure he saw slithering down the sand was his Uncle Tom. Then, almost the next moment, standing at the top of the rise leading into the copse, he saw Brid's mother. Funny, but he had never called her Aunty Alice. She shouted now, calling, 'John! Come and help me down, John.'

When his father hurried forward and began to climb the rise, Sandy turned back to the schoolteacher. This was one he could handle.

'Think you're clever, don't you?' His features converged to a point and seemed to pierce the teacher's face. 'You forget that people leave school. You want to mind your own bloody business.' There was a sing-song quality to his voice, and the teacher recognised it as a prelude. This was the way this type talked before an attack, but he knew that Sandy Palmer would not attack him at this moment. Yet he knew also that he wasn't finished with Sandy Palmer, or, more correctly, Sandy Palmer wasn't finished with him. He would likely suffer for defending the boy back there in the water. Well, let him start anything. The anger was strong in him now, strong as it had been when he first heard his nickname. Just let him start anything and he would have him along the line for as many years as it was possible for him to get. Just let him try anything on him. Just let him. He felt his heartbeats quickening, his stomach contracting, and the muscles of his shoulders hardening, and he thought, The dirty bastard. He had a desire to spring on this boy and pound his fists into the thin leering face, the face that was a portrait of evil in its essence if he had ever seen it, the face that nothing in this life would be able to alter for the better . . . Redemption. The word presented itself to him and he literally almost spat it out of his mouth, and his mind answered it as if it had been voiced by another, saying, Who are you talking to? Redemption . . . and this. I've been dealing with them for twenty-eight years, don't forget. If Christ Himself came and laid his hands on him he would be unable to make him clean. Here, he actually shook his head as if answering the voice, Aw! Don't talk to me.

He came to himself with a voice calling 'Brid!' and before turning his attention to the woman who was shouting, he thought for a moment, Let him try anything on, just let him. The woman was now standing at the edge of the water with the man Palmer and she was calling, 'Brid! Brid!' Sandy Palmer did not go near them and not one of the three seemed to bother about the man running along the sands.

When the man stumbled past the teacher he was gasping, and he spoke between great gulps of air to the woman's back, crying, 'Think you're clever, eh? Think you're clever.' He did not look at the teacher. He did not bring him into the focus of this family affair. He was looking at his wife and his pal, and now at his pal's son. Then going to the receding line of the tide and raising his hands to his mouth, he yelled, 'Come here you! Come here! Do you hear me?'

'Shut up!'

'What! What did you say?'

The two men were looking at each other straight in the eye for the first time in years, and John Palmer repeated, 'I said, shut up! I'm going to deal with this, I've told you. It's me that's going to deal with it.'

'Be God! you are. Be God! you are.'

'Yes, I am, Tom.' John Palmer's voice had dropped swiftly to a quiet, reasonable tone. 'And listen, there's something about this that I just don't get. Brid isn't in her bare skin, nor the lad. An' there's a woman out there with them.'

'That's my wife.'

They all turned towards the teacher and he, some-what puzzled, went on, 'I don't know what you mean by bare skin; the girl has never been in her bare skin, not to my knowledge. I have told this man here how I came upon them.' He nodded towards John. 'And it's lucky I did, or else this one' – he indicated Sandy Palmer – 'might be in a police van at this minute. And my opinion is that's where he should be.'

Tom and Alice Stevens, their attention pulled from the water for the moment, stared at the man. To them he might have been talking German, but not so to John Palmer. And when Sandy advanced towards the teacher, muttering, 'Mind! I've told you. If you don't keep your tongue—' his father barked, 'Hold your hand! An' keep your tongue quiet and them fists down or else I'll deal with you an' all.'

'What's this? What's this, anyway?' Alice Stevens looked from one to the other in a bemused way. 'I thought we came here to fetch Brid. Look, whatever it is, we'll sort it out after.' She turned now and called with a beseeching note in her voice, 'Here! Brid. Come here, I tell you. I want you.'

The tide was no longer lapping over the top of the rocks. Brid was sitting stiff and straight as she looked across the bay towards her family. There seemed to be coming over the water from them a density of feeling: all the hate, subtlety, pretence, anxiety, frustration that had existed between the two families for years came at her. Her own share of these emotions had been pretence and anxiety. Anxiety had become a recognised part of her existence. The feeling was so strong now that she wanted to retch into the water.

Joe Lloyd swam up to her unnoticed, and when he put his hand on her knee she jumped as if his touch had burned her.

'Don't be frightened. What are you frightened about? You've done nothing. Come on. Come on back to them. I'll go with you.'

'No. No. I'm not going. Not now. I'm not going back, I'm not, I'm not.'

'Don't worry, don't agitate yourself.' It was the woman speaking. She put her hand on Brid's shoulder and Brid turned to her swiftly as if to her mother and said, 'They can't make me, can they? They can't make me.'

'Nobody can make you do anything you don't want to.' She became concerned: the girl was terrified of something or someone, likely that Palmer individual. She looked towards the shore and she herself began to feel nervous. She wished Len would come back.

The group on the beach waited.

Alice Stevens said helplessly now, 'What can we do if she won't come?' She was speaking to John but it was her husband who answered. 'She can't stay out for ever, that's a certainty, and I can wait.'

At his words she drooped her head for a moment, then put her hand inside her coat and gripped at her breast. And then her attention was brought again to the strange man. The teacher was in the water up to his knees and was facing them. 'What do you want her for, what has she done?' he said. 'Why can't you leave her alone?'

'Look here, you! This is none of your business. I don't know who the hell you are, so keep out of it if you know what's good for you. I've stood enough.'

The teacher addressed himself solely to Tom as he answered, 'I'd say it was my business, I've been thrust into it. I've told you. And my advice to you is leave her alone. She's doing no harm. She's having a swim with her boy-friend. Is there anything wrong in that?'

The word boy-friend seemed to have an electrifying effect on Sandy Palmer, for it was at this point that he began stripping himself of his clothes, tearing them off, and his father, turning quickly and looking at him, said, 'What are you up to?'

Sandy was now stepping out of his trousers. He left on his short pants. His body was skinny yet appeared to be hard and wiry. He looked back at his father. 'You want her out, don't you? You came in a bus load to get her. Well, if she won't come on her own, she's got to be made to, hasn't she? That's all.'

'Look; you stay where you are.' John Palmer moved from the group and towards his son, and Sandy, backing from him, said fiercely, 'You try an' stop me—' then under his breath, he finished, 'you and her and him,' and on this, he swung about and plunged into the water.

At the first sight of Sandy Palmer stripping himself, the teacher had turned from the group and made rapidly for the rocks again. Alone, he was aware he would be no match for the Palmer hooligan, but with the lad out there, and his wife not a bad third, he would be able effectively to stop him scaring that girl to death.

John Palmer was now standing in the water seemingly unconscious of his shoes being flooded. Then without looking at his feet he lifted his knees and, having loosened one shoe after the other, threw them back on the beach. He would have followed his son whether or not Alice Stevens had beseeched him, 'Yes, you go, John. You go and fetch her. She won't come for Sandy.'

'Look here! If there's anybody goin''—' Tom Stevens moved towards the water's edge, but the water had only covered the rims of his shoes before his wife's scathing voice hit him and he knew that the situation had suddenly gone out of his control. Her voice even told him that he had never controlled any part of it.

'Don't be so bloody soft,' she said; 'you can't swim an inch; you know you can't.'

The truth bent his shoulders for a moment and made him shrivel up, and he stepped back into line with her and watched his friend swimming after his son . . .

Joe was still near Brid's knees. When he stretched his toes down he could feel the bottom now; in a few minutes he would be able to stand up. With her and the woman he watched the teacher swimming towards them. He had heard the voices on the beach but could not make out what they were saying. But he saw clearly the figure of Sandy Palmer stripping off his clothes.

When the teacher was alongside them he stood up and turned round to ascertain the distance that Palmer had yet to make before reaching them, and he drew a great gulp of air into his lungs before saying, 'He means trouble. Now look.' He cast his eyes up and back at his wife: 'I don't like the idea of us being stuck up there. The tide's going down fast and if we can stand on our feet we'll be able to manage him better. Come on.' He held out his hand towards Brid. 'Don't be frightened. We won't let him get near you. I don't know what all this is about. Have you done something or other? Been up to something?'

She shook her head swiftly, and then said, 'Me? . . . Me? No. Nothing. I've done nothing.'

'Well, I don't know.' He sighed. 'Anyway, come down.'

As his wife was slipping down from the rock into the water, he put up his hand towards Brid's arm while Joe's hand went out to take her other arm; but she pulled back quickly from them, saying, 'No!

I'm not going. I'm not going. I'm not going back while they're there. I tell you I'm not.'

'But you can't stay here all the time.' It was Joe speaking. He coaxed now, 'Look, Sandy Palmer can't touch us. There are other people there. He wouldn't dare. And anyway he's not got me alone now, the shoe's on the other foot. Just let him try anything. Come on, come on down before he gets here.'

She pulled her feet up from out of the water and under her, and edged further back on the flat piece of rock; and the teacher, speaking now with a touch of irritation and even anger in his voice, said, 'Look, don't be foolish. Come down off there.' He even made to clamber up on the rock, when the grip of his wife's hand on his arm turned him about and he followed the direction of her eyes to where Sandy Palmer was changing his course and was making for the rocks to the side of them. And as they watched him they knew his intention. Brid was on the rocks and that was where he was going. He had only to clamber up further along and if his feet could withstand the jagged edges he would presently be in an advantageous position. With this thought in both their minds, Joe and the school teacher immediately pulled themselves up beside Brid, although the woman remained in the water.

When Sandy Palmer stood balancing himself on the sloping surface of rocks, he addressed himself to Brid, shouting as if she were miles away, 'Well, are you coming back, or do I have to fetch you?' She did not answer, but, scrambling to her feet, she stood up between Joe and the teacher, and it was Joe who answered for her. 'Come and try and get her.' A pause followed this, and then Joe added, 'She doesn't want to come out and if she doesn't want to come out she's not comin'! You understand?' Joe was bending forward, his teeth bared. There was an overwhelming desire in him to bridge the distance with a leap, for he was feeling Palmer's breath on his face once again and seeing the cigarette sticking to the skin of his lower lip. The burn under his trunks began to smart furiously.

Sandy Palmer stared back at Joe and his words were carried on the dark gleam of his eyes. 'I'll deal with you after. In the meantime, shut your gob if you know what's good for you. Haven't you had enough?'

'Get down off there!'

The voice from the water startled them all except the woman, and they looked to where John Palmer was standing at the foot of the rocks, his feet on the sand and his head well above the water now.

'You keep out of this; it's none of your business. I've told you.' Sandy Palmer was bending towards his father, and they stared at each other for a moment before he added, 'Aye, but I suppose you would say it was your business. But you've left it a bit late, eh? What d'you think? You haven't had the guts to tell her . . . well, I'm goin' to tell her.'

'Come down out of that.' John Palmer's voice sounded steady, even untroubled, so untroubled that, under the circumstances, it was more frightening. For answer Sandy spat into the water, then moved towards Brid and the two men flanking her. So steady was his approach that he could have been walking on a flat surface, and his unhesitating advance caused a spasm of fear in both Joe and the teacher. Sandy Palmer was a bully, a coward at heart, and yet the teacher recognised in some inscrutable way that he was now being driven by a force of which bravery was the weakest element. Nothing could stop him from coming at them and getting his hands on this girl.

Sandy Palmer stopped when he was just over a yard from them, and his father's voice beat at him now as he made ready to spring. 'Sandy! D'you hear me? . . . Sandy!' As John Palmer pulled himself on to his knees on the rocks just to the side of the teacher he almost fell back into the water again, for Brid let rip a scream. The next moment she had jumped backwards. It was like a child doing hopscotch, and her legs meeting with John's head as he made to rise sent her sprawling. Within a split second and another scream she was in the frothing water on the ocean side of the rocks.

The tide all the time had been gushing, rushing and hissing through the crevices. The surface of the water behind the rocks was bubbling and churning and creating a froth. They knelt on the rocks and strained and reached out to her, but when she went whirling and dizzying from them Joe stood up, then dived. But there was no accountable period of time between his outstretched arms hitting the water and those of Sandy Palmer.

Joe had hold of Brid. One minute he was seeing the white faces capping the black rocks and the next minute the far horizon was bobbing before his eyes. They went twisting and turning time and again before his efforts brought them anywhere near the rocks. He wasn't conscious of Sandy Palmer being in the water until the hands came down from the rocks and grabbed at Brid. It was when he was relieved of her weight that the hand clutched his ribs, and he was spun round and down. For one terrifying moment all the churning, boiling water in the sea seemed to be racing down his throat, and when, spluttering and coughing, he slit the surface he could see nothing for the salt in his eyes. But he knew that Sandy Palmer was near him. He thrashed at the swirling water, and as his vision cleared and he saw the rocks before him he felt the grab again, at his leg this time. As he twirled and twisted and kicked out there was a fearsome screeching terror ripping through him in all directions. Sandy Palmer was trying to drown him. He came up again, and now he was quite near the rocks and there were hands outstretched to him, and he grabbed at them and caught them. But the hold was on his legs once more, like being in the grip of a revolving

174

steel hawser. His body was being stretched again. It was like torture, just as it had been when he was tied to the trees. This was his lot. This was the end. Palmer was going to make sure of him . . . Oh! Christ . . . An almost insufferable agony went through his brain as his hair was gripped and his scalp pulled upwards. There were nails digging into his shoulders; there were hands around his throat. His face was close to the rock and he was being torn in two. Then the steel girder snapped and he was free, and his body was catapulted up the face of the rock and he was lying gasping and panting and spluttering on top of the teacher and his wife.

John Palmer was still kneeling on the rocks. He was breathing hard as if he himself was actually battling with the current. When he saw his son's head appear amid the froth, the words, like a prayer, were wrenched from the depth of his bowels and he cried, 'Oh God, if only he would drown.' But it was a futile prayer, for his son could swim like a fish. What was more, he had always been able to stay under water for long periods. Hadn't they just witnessed what he could do under water? He had stayed down long enough to attempt to pull another lad to his death. No one would ever have any proof. Even this teacher fellow and his wife could not say that it was his son's hand that had held the lad down. They could think as much, and surmise as much, but only he would know. For was it not he himself who had first introduced him to this water game, diving under him and tweeking his toes? Sandy was about seven at the time. When he was ten he could turn the tables effectively and haul him under, as big as he was.

Sandy was yards out now from the rocks. Strong swimmer that he was, the submersion under such conditions had taken it out of him. He made for the rocks again, swimming hard against the pull of the water, and when he was within a couple of breast strokes from them he looked up to see his father staring down at him, and he twisted into a position of treading water. Even in this turbulent spray he had the control to do that. It was only for a flashing second that he saw the look in his father's eyes, but it was long enough to tell him there were no secrets of any kind between them any more.

The feeling that John Palmer had for his son at this moment went beyond hate and horror. It went beyond self-analysis. What this boy possessed was what he had put into him. Not in a moment of passion – he could in a way have understood it then – but in a duty-filled moment, a Friday-night habit. That fact at least should have bred some sort of ordinariness, should have bred a boy cut out to a decent pattern. Bred out of duty, and without passion, and brought up respectably. Nor had he known hardship or want, the two spurs that made men different, that created so many different urges. Sandy had known none of these things and yet he was different, frighteningly different. Scaringly different. Repulsively different. Hatefully different.

John Palmer was oblivious now to the turmoil on the rock. The commotion going on to the side of him seemed to be of no concern to him. He stared at his son, who was now making to swim with the current and towards his right, where the rocks were more easy of access. His gaze followed him. Without moving his body he kept his eyes on him. He knew what he was going to do once he had him up on top. He felt his fingers moving into a fist. He could already feel the shock going through his system with the contact of his knuckles between his son's eyes, and that would only be the beginning. Although he was aware that he could never knock out of his son what was in him, he knew he would have to make a show of trying. He saw that he was now about fifteen feet away to the side of him, and not more than two yards away from the rocks. One minute he was watching him swimming, the next he was watching him bobbing and splashing and thrashing with his arms. Then he saw him spin round. It was as if someone had got hold of him and was twisting his body into a corkscrew. He uttered a sound that was like the screech of a terrified animal. It was cut off abruptly, smothered in the twisting.

When John Palmer saw his son twist again in that odd way he sprang up from his knees and jumped along from the top of one rock to the other until he was opposite him. He saw him spin again, helplessly now, and he flung himself flat on the rock into a position from where he could stretch out his hands to him. There was a split second when his long arm could have reached the flailing arms of the boy, but it passed. His fingers seemed locked in the crevices of the rocks below his chest. He remained motionless, as he watched Sandy's body being whirled away over the gut to the quicksands beyond.

When he heard the groan to the side of him he knew it came from the teacher fellow, and he dropped his face forward until his chin touched the rock, and he did not lift it even when the man yelled at him, 'Can't you do something? Look, I'll go in, hang on to me.'

Then John Palmer's fingers were released from the rock and he grabbed at the region of the man's ribs, then worked them upwards to his arm and gripped it. And when he spoke there was froth around his mouth. 'It's no use, it's . . . it's the undercurrent; you'd only be sucked in.'

'God Almighty!' The teacher had had a final glimpse of the face of the boy who had given him the name of Farty Morley. It was a terrified face. White, bleached, horrible, already without flesh. It showed for one second longer and then was gone. There had been no shouting or crying. The fear that Sandy Palmer had instilled into others had turned on him and he had gone under, paralysed by his own weapon.

'Oh God. Oh God Almighty!' The teacher forgot that he hated Sandy Palmer; he could only think of him being sucked down by the undercurrent. And again he said, 'Oh God. Oh God,' and the sound of his voice seemed to echo across the water. As he looked at the sun almost blinding him with its reflection on the waves, he thought. It can't be, it can't be. The whole thing, the whole day, had taken on an atmosphere of nightmare, and it wasn't until the man at his feet groaned that this feeling was dispelled.

John Palmer was standing now and looking into the frothing surface of the water. There was no hole left to show that his son had passed through that surface ... And the sins of the fathers will be visited upon the children, even to the third and fourth generation. Well, there would be no chance of a third or fourth generation through Sandy, he had made sure of that. A thought hit him with the shock of a bullet in the chest: he could have saved him, he could, he could. But he had let him drown. The rising panic in him was quelled by a steadying voice which said, Better so, better so. He was no good. He would have done for her; one way or the other he would have done for her. I've always known that, he thought He brought his head slowly round and looked along the jagged pinnacle of rocks. He could see the lad lying flat on his face and the woman next to him, and she had her arms about Brid and Brid was yelling. His daughter was yelling and struggling. He brought his gaze back to the strange man who was looking at him, his face convulsed with pity, and as he was about to speak, John Palmer put out his hand and said, 'Say nothing . . . Not now. Say nothing.'

The teacher's wife now called, 'Len! here a minute! Help me,' and he scrambled over the rocks towards her with a slightly drunken gait. He too was feeling tired, and sick.

Brid was still struggling in the woman's arms and talking incoherently, and when Len tried to restrain her struggles, she screamed louder. It brought Joe into full consciousness again, and he turned on his elbow and raised himself a little. When, between the jerking movements of her head she saw him, her screaming dropped into a whimper, and her struggles ceased and she said with a semblance of rationality, 'Joe. Oh Joe. I thought you were . . . Oh Joe.' She fell towards him and put her arms around him as she might have done if they were alone.

Pulling himself up into a sitting position he held her, and Len knelt at his back and supported him. The woman stood up. She seemed thankful for a moment's respite from Brid's struggles and as she looked towards John Palmer he spoke to her quietly, his voice, again terrifyingly ordinary, saying, 'I'm going on out; will you bring her?' He did not wait for an answer, and she offered none, but she watched him slide into the water and wade towards the shore. The water now was below his chest. She looked at her husband and asked impatiently, 'Where's the other one?'

He swallowed and for once was lost for words. The voluble teacher was lost for words. With a trembling hand he thumbed the tumbling foam behind him, and his wife put her fingers across her mouth as she muttered, 'No! No!'

Joe put his head well back now to look up at the teacher, and his words sounded as thick as those of a drunken man as he said, 'You mean he's . . . that he's—?' The word ended on a high note, right up at the back of his throat. And when the man did not answer him he drooped his head and stared at Brid. But she was not looking at him; she had her face buried in her hands, and her hands were resting on his knees. He couldn't take it in. It couldn't be true that Palmer was dead. Dead . . . Drowned. That's what he had tried to do to him, drown *him*. He began to shake, trembling from the crown of his head to the nails on his toes. The experience that had been dimmed for a moment in semi-consciousness was back. He could feel the grip on his ankle, he could feel the two hands clawing at his legs. He looked over Brid's head towards his feet. There'd be marks on his ankles. That grip would have surely left marks, but he couldn't see them because of Brid's head. He was shaking so violently now that his teeth began to chatter and a strange voice from behind him said, 'You've got to get them in.' When he was pulled to his feet Brid still clung to him and wouldn't let him go, and when they tried to get her off him she yelled, and he said like a stuttering man, 'Le–le–leave her b–be.'

And like this, they waded slowly towards the shore.

Meanwhile John Palmer was facing Tom and Alice Stevens, and, without any preamble, he said in a quiet, even deadly-sounding voice, 'Sandy's gone, caught in the undercurrent.'

'What!' The word came screeching out of Alice. 'What? Dead! My God! Olive'll go mad. He was all she had.'

'Yes; you saw to that.'

'What!' Again the screech. 'You're blamin' me for all this, when it's that damned lad, that maniac that got Brid out at four in the morning? My God! And poor Sandy dead . . . blaming me!'

'Well, there's one thing for sure. If he hadn't drowned, he would have been in prison before long, on a charge of torture.'

'Torture? What are you sayin'?'

'I'm sayin', this very afternoon he headed his pals and tortured that lad there.' He thumbed to where Len was supporting Joe's back against a rock. 'They stripped him naked, tied him, spreadeagled, to trees, and my son burned him with a blazing cigarette. I leave you to guess where. Only God knows what would have happened if Brid had not arrived on the scene and her screams hadn't brought that teacher and his wife up from the beach here, where they had been bathing. The wife, being a nurse, thought the best thing for them both was to get them into the water to calm them down, for they were both in a state.'

'Huh! He couldn't have been all that bad, when he could bash young Talbot as he did,' said Tom Stevens.

'Well, from what this man tells me, that happened later when young Talbot arrived, meaning to join the gang. What he saw was young Brid naked. She was with that woman behind a bush, getting into her bathing costume. And this lad saw him, and then went at him mad, like.'

'I don't believe it,' Alice said. 'Anyway, she's coming home,' and she thrust past John and made for her daughter, where she was kneeling beside Joe.

'Come away from there; you're coming home.'

Brid sprang to her feet, yelling, 'I'm not! I'm not! Never! Not to you three!'

The men were now lined alongside Alice, and Brid cried again, 'I'm not! Never! You're filthy . . . rotten, all of you!'

'Rotten we may be, but I brought you up.' This was a bark from Tom. 'I'm your father . . .' he was saying, only to be thrust back by John's arm, and his yelling, 'You're not her father, and she knows it. I'm her father, and from now on I'm acting like it, and if she says she doesn't want to come back among us rotten lot, she's not comin' back, she's goin' her own road.'

'By God! she's not.' Alice's arm was thrust out to make a grab at Brid, only for Len and his wife to react together to shield her, the while John, gripping Alice by the shoulder, thrust her well back.

The three stood staring at each other, and for what was next said, they could have been in the privacy of one or the other's house, for in that odd quiet voice John said, 'This is final. It's the finish; and not before time. We are movin'—' he was staring at Alice. 'I should have done it years ago. You, Alice, are like a disease that has to be hidden, and it gets worse with the years. You blackmailed me because of Brid; and you, Tom, like a worm, you took it. Oh! don't put your fists up at me. I could have floored you years ago; and I could do it this minute, not because I've detested your guts, but because of the weals that are showing up on my daughter's shoulder and neck. And they are not strap weals, they were caused by chains.'

'Yes, they're from chain,' Tom Stevens came back at him. 'I, too, should have done it earlier. I wish I had now.'

John Palmer remained quiet for a moment. His teeth were clenched; then he said, 'Try practising it on the one who deserves it. And good luck to you, for you'll have only each other now, for what you mightn't yet know is, the two lads are setting up on their own; they've taken a flat. Yes, as Brid said, we're a mucky lot.'

Alice Stevens was standing now, her eyes wide, her lips stretched from her teeth, her whole body taut as if ready to spring. 'You swine, you!' She had brought out the words through tight lips. 'I could kill you meself, this very minute. You're a dirty, cowardly swine.'

'Yes; yes, perhaps I am. It seems I've always known that. But there was your laugh. Laugh everything off, that was your motto, wasn't it? while you drove your poor bugger of a husband mad. The only thing I'll say in my defence now is, I am not proud of that part of it.' He cast a rather pitying glance towards his one-time pal, before saying, 'You can take her home now because I'm goin' to see that Brid goes where she wants to, and that's with that lad.'

He was about to turn away when he paused and said, 'By the way, it'll be in the papers the morrer that my son was drowned while trying to save a fellow swimmer. That's, of course, if the lad agrees to it. If he doesn't, all the muck will come out, and you wouldn't like that, would you, Alice? So be careful what you say when you get back there.'

John now turned and addressed himself to Len, saying, 'Have you a car?'

Stiffly, Len replied, 'Yes, I have a car; it's behind Morgan's garage.'

'Well, I would get it, and get the lad home.'

For a moment, Len did not reply; but he turned to his wife and said, 'Bring their clothes down, and anything else you can carry. Then go and get the car.'

The woman nodded, but before obeying her husband, she ran towards a group of small rocks where she picked up a linen skirt, into which she stepped before pulling on a sleeveless blouse. And with this, John Palmer turned to Brid, where she was again kneeling by Joe's side, and he said quietly, 'You want to go with the lad, Brid?'

Her face had worn a grim, defiant look, almost of hate, as she looked at him, but his kindly tone softened her reply: 'Yes, I do, and . . .' she paused, 'for always.'

'Good enough. There's nobody goin' to stop you. I'll see to that.'

Then turning to the Stevenses, he said, 'I'd get away if I were you, because I'm not movin' until they're in that car.'

'Twenty-eight,' Joe called from the back seat of the car, where he and Brid were sitting close and supporting each other; and Mrs Morley, looking out of the car window, said, 'Yes; it should be the next one;' and straightway she said, 'Here! Len.'

When the car stopped opposite the green-painted door, Len and Phyllis got out quickly. While Len was helping Joe to alight, his wife was knocking on the house door.

When Mrs Lloyd opened the door and saw her son standing there, being supported, it would seem, by a strange man, and a tousled-haired girl being assisted by a woman, she exclaimed, 'Oh! Dear God, what's happened? What's happened to you?'

'It's all right, Mother. It's all right.'

As his mother banged the door closed behind them, Joe did not make for the kitchen door, but turned his shaking steps down the short passage and led them into the sitting-room and, staggering, he made his way to the chintz-covered couch and dropped on to it.

Lying back, he closed his eyes for a second, and said on a gasp, 'Brid . . . rest. Sit down.'

As Phyllis helped Brid lower herself into an easy chair, Mary Lloyd kept repeating, 'What is it? What's happened?' And she bent over Joe now, saying, 'Where are you hurt?'

When Joe did not answer, Len put in, 'There's been a bit of trouble, Mrs Lloyd. I'll explain presently.'

'Mother' – Joe's voice was pleading – 'go and mash some tea. Take . . . take my friends with you.' He hadn't paused on the use of 'friends', but added, 'They'll explain.'

'But . . . but—'

'Mother; please! I'm all in at the moment. I'd . . .
I'd like a cup of tea. Go on now . . . go on.' He gave a
weak wave of his hand after pushing her off, and she
backed slowly from him as if reluctant to go. She then
looked at the two strangers and said weakly, 'Will you
. . . will you come this way?'

When the click of the door came to Brid, where she
was leaning her head in the corner of the high-back
chair, she opened her eyes and looked across at Joe;
then pulling herself up from the chair, she dropped on
to her knees beside the couch, whispering now, 'Oh!
Joe . . . Joe.'

'It's all right. It's all over,' and he put an arm around
her shoulders, and she laid her head on his chest for a
moment. But her tenderness did not quell the terror
and shivering that was in his body, and of which
he imagined he would never be free, for he could
still feel the snakelike grip of Sandy Palmer's hand
on his ankle, dragging him down, round and round,
dragging him deeper and deeper, never to rise again.
He had thought he could never experience greater fear
than when he had lain for seven hours behind a fall
in the pit, and he'd had company there; three others
were with him. But the terror of the time he had been
in that maniac's hold was beyond anything he could
explain in words.

As if Brid had picked up his thoughts, she now
whimpered, 'I'm still terrified, Joe. I know he's dead,

but I can't stop shaking inside. I'm frightened now that, in some way, she'll come and take me back.'

He made an effort and pulled himself further up the couch so that he could hold her with both arms; and his voice had the comfort of his old assurance: 'Oh no, she won't,' he said. 'That man . . . the other man who said he is your father, he won't let them. He's different. Anyway, I'll see that they don't come near you. You'll never need to be afraid any more. Here you are, and here you'll stay.'

'But . . . but your mother.'

'She knows all about you. I told her before I left the house this afternoon that you were for me.' And now he added, 'You are, aren't you?'

'Oh, yes, Joe. Yes, Joe.' She put a hand on his cheek. 'I . . . I love you. I seem to have known you for years. But where will I stay until—?'

'You'll stay here, my love . . . here, until we're married. And that can be soon.'

'Will your mother not mind?'

'No; she'll be glad. Now she can marry her grocer. She's been waiting to do so, but I've been the stumbling-block. She wouldn't leave me here on my own. Now she'll go to his house, and we'll live here.'

'Oh! Joe. Joe . . . I . . . I can't believe it.'

'You can believe it all right, my Brid.'

On these last words his mother came back in to the

room. She had one hand tightly over her mouth; she had been crying. And when she came to the couch, he held out his hand to her, and she took it. Then she lifted her eyes from him to the kneeling girl, and put her other hand on Brid's head, and stroked the still damp hair.

They looked at each other, and in their gaze, they both saw the years ahead.

And now, looking at her son, Mary Lloyd said, 'I've mashed the tea. Your friends are staying for a cup. They are a nice couple. Do you think you can make it to the kitchen? Come along, lass.' She held out her hand.